SUGAR MUMMY

Confessions
of a
Sugar Mummy

Emma Tennant

GIBSON SQUARE

By the same author

To the friend who reminded me of the saying
'Dying is easy. Comedy is hard'.

This edition first published in 2007 by

Gibson Square
47 Lonsdale Square
London N1 1EW
UK

UK Tel: ++44 (0)20 7096 1100
    Fax: ++44 (0)20 7993 2214

US Tel: ++1 646 216 9813
    Fax: ++1 646 216 9488

Eire Tel: ++353 (0)1 657 1057

info@gibsonsquare.com
www.gibsonsquare.com

ISBN 978-1906142018 (1906142017)

Printed by Clays Ltd

Index

Confessions

OF

A SUGAR MUMMY

The Object of Desire

☋ 1 ☋

You might ask what a woman in her sixties wants—a question Freud forgot to ask. What do women want? he wrote, but it's possible, like most people, he didn't see women in their sixties as women at all, so it wasn't worth trying to find out.

I certainly have had Sugar Mummy proclivities for a long time. (And I know it's a common affliction, although most Mummies keep quiet about it.) Seen an old woman forcing stale bread into a reluctant duck in the park?—she's a thwarted Sugar Mummy, too repressed to swap the duck for a Younger Man, too nervous of rejection to turn the soggy bread into gold and go shopping at Browns with him for an entire new wardrobe (for him, of course). It's a nerve-wracking business, being old-enough-to-be-his-mother. At least Freud touched on that with the Oedipus complex. It was just that he never bothered to try and look at the situation from the point of view of the poor innocent incest-provider's mother, Jocasta. Did she get what she wanted from the stranger who showed up one day and then turned out to be her son? Did she at least have a good time for a while?

I'll tell you how it happened for me. Compared to the tragic queen of myth, I'm a straightforward case: Alain is not my son, he's no relation. Apart from waiters—'Would your son like the bill, Madam?' and drivers of expensive cars hired to take us round London in search of property to buy (don't ask)—who expected me to wait in the car (too old to get in and out quickly) while Alain skipped up vertiginous steps, I was really pretty free of obnoxious comments.

But then, why should there be any? The joke is, I'm in my sixties and Alain is his forties. He's twenty years younger, but maddeningly he looks young (unless he's been drinking)—but older women aren't in a strong enough position to remark on that, because getting someone to the doctor is the primrose path to actual motherhood.

Alain has dark hair—if there's any grey I'm blind to it—and he's French/Polish/Jewish, which appears to me to be an irresistible combination: there's the French, which to a woman of my generation means embarrassing memories of being seventeen in Paris and wearing dresses in the 1950s that were all whalebone and artificial flowers; there's the Polish, which is somehow Roman Polanski and *Knife in the Water* and the promise of sex; and there's the Jewish, which is better than Freud at understanding exactly what you want and even helping you to get it. The fact that Alain doesn't live up to any of these expectations is one of the main problems faced, I'm pretty certain, by every Sugar Mummy.

How can someone with all these romantic origins fail—except perhaps at being French (but actually he does fail there because, as I discovered, he isn't really French at all, just had a French stepmother and after the age of seven went to live with his father's brother in London). The sex and the deep psychoanalytical grip on what I'm like look as if they're frankly not going to happen…

So how did I get hooked on Alain? Am I likely to survive the orgies of spending, the guilt and the sickening feeling he doesn't want half the things I buy or do for him anyway?

It happened through—don't laugh—interior decoration. I do a bit of doing up people's houses and then I sell them on—and it was in Bandol in the south of France that I met Alain—and, yes, his wife Claire. They live in the kind of fabulous place you see in the Sunday supplements. A *mas* and out-buildings all set round a courtyard, vines spreading away in front, pine trees, view of the sea, the lot. Alain and Claire make terracotta pots and tiles, and I went there last year to find something for a flat I was doing up in Nice.

The best way to summarise the lunch is to set out a list of rules, what to do and not do when you know you're about to become a Sugar Mummy:

If you feel an instant attraction (as I did that day in the south of France) don't sit staring at your prey—I can't think of a better word—all the way through the meal his wife provides. Look interested only in the pots and tiles—at my age it's all you're allowed to be interested in anyway. (Or maybe the latest P D James crime novel: old ladies are supposed to like crime.)

Do *not* try to make an assignation. It will be met with a blank stare.

On no account rush to the loo and apply Touche Eclat or whatever the ruinously expensive foundation is called, the one that claims to remove your wrinkles and fill in the vertical lines down to your mouth, the result of a fifty-year nicotine habit. You will look strangely different, it's true, but certainly not for the better, as they claim.

Ditto with bright lipstick. The aforementioned lines just love racing down from your nose to meet a streak of scarlet that's already smudged on wrinkled skin.

Don't stare at the pot belly which has mysteriously recently appeared. Wear a loose-fitting garment—yes, it's depressing, but the 'bump that stills desire' really does do just that.

♋   ♋   ♋   ♋

So there you are, Alain the handsome, Claire the lovely, hard-working wife (she makes all the pots, Alain makes the odd tile) and it's only as we're picking at pears in a wonderful red wine syrup that I begin to understand that this perfect couple are deep in the shit (as those less refined than Alain and Claire would say).

They are stony broke. Claire's half-brother is the owner of the fabulous *mas* and he's remarrying next month. He wants Alain and Claire out of the place.

They'll have to move and they've nowhere to go. Pots and tiles, however tasteful, won't pay the rent.

I didn't know then why I was let in on all this, but maybe I do now. 'I will show you my new designs when I come to London next week', Alain says. He has a great line in the self-deprecating shrug and smile, and I literally felt my heart turn over.

'Yes, I'm looking for some tiles', I ad lib. 'A big house in… in Holland Park…'

'So I'll come and see you', Alain says.

That was how I crossed the line from someone wearing old shoes (how *could* I have not bought new sandals before I came out here?) to a hobbling wreck in totally unaffordable Manolos.

But I had to do it. I had become a Sugar Mummy.

House Lift, Face Lift

∽ 2 ∽

What is it about this part of London? It has a trendy name, 'Maida Hill', which makes it sound like Maida Vale on speed. It's described as being 'close to the bars and restaurants of Notting Hill', but, however many Hills get thrown at it, the grid of dreary grey streets stays just the same year after year: the Land Time Forgot.

I live on the ground and basement floors of a house someone tried to gentrify about thirty years ago. Like the rest of the neighbourhood, with its betting shops, unappealing pubs and occasional corner shops selling identical frozen foods and redtops, it has an apologetic, 'tired' look (the estate agents' favourite word when viewing property round here). Abandon hope all ye who live in a bedsit in this region, the place seems to say—and the funny thing is that, despite the Moroccan carpets, the Balinese chandeliers and the multicoloured cord from Crucial Trading, my flat still looks like a bedsit and I've got to look temporary as well.

But now is the time of change. My face is going to go up—I don't care how much it costs—and just as I'm deciding this the prices go up round here as well.

I've never had money (if I make it, it's blown while the bank is still putting it in my account) and I'm amazed when the letters and cards and other junk mail start coming through my letterbox. Suddenly my flat is worth a fortune—and there are boards all the way down the street as well, offering the previously despised houses and maisonettes and broom cupboards for hundreds and hundreds of thousands of pounds. I mean, I can take a minicab down to Notting Hill and choose the trattoria of my dreams—on paper at least I'm worth half a million pounds.

Of course all this leads to major fantasising about my future with Alain. I run over in my head the obvious drawbacks to a love affair. Why would a man who already has an older wife—although she doesn't look it, the lovely Claire is ten years older than he is—leave her for an even older woman? Answer: why indeed?

Then there's worry over the logistics of my wonderful coming life as a rich woman. If this dump has gone up overnight like a magic mushroom, then where am I—and, I add to myself a shade coyly, perhaps Alain—going to live when this is sold for a staggering sum? Won't everywhere be the same? (But no, comes another reassuring answer: all at once this has become a 'prime area' close to Julia Roberts and Hugh Grant and all the world's bankers. Maida Hill will soon be Notting itself into zillion-pound properties—hooray!)

It doesn't take me long to realise there's a real undercurrent of anxiety in my jubilation. And it takes me all morning and a trip to the still-depressing local Patel (I can see the coming deli with the prosciutto and the mango ice-cream and tables on the pavement with people drinking a latte or kir, but it sure ain't happened yet) to work out what's gnawing at my vitals.

It's this: what will Alain want to do with my money? Start a tile business? God I hope not: the picture of bank-busting lorries carrying terracotta tiles across Europe plus the rents in boutiques in

Kensington where the bloody things will lie unsold for months on end simply brings me out in a sweat. Yet he can't do nothing… or can he? Didn't I fall for his lazy charm a whole week ago in Bandol? Couldn't he just… stay at home in bed with me?

My reverie was broken by a phone call from Harvey Nicks. I'd called the Beauty Department earlier and had a fascinating chat with Georgina there, who told me firmly that surgery was so yesterday and she had the creams and 'fillers' for the bomb crater that looks back at me in the mirror every day.

'Maida Hill?' Georgina says and she sounds impressed—the first time anyone has reacted in this way to where I live. 'I can come over with a selection, madam, I'll be with you by twelve.'

So it is that I admitted Georgina to my newly desirable abode, home of a happy Sugar Mummy with plenty of hope and smiles. 'My mother swears by this cream for under the eyes', says the guileless Georgina, and I have to hope she doesn't see my smile turn to a scowl, which of course leads to a deepening of those lines around the mouth and a sag in the jaw that resembles a collapsing sponge. 'I'll try it', I say, gallant to the last. Georgina may think I'm no more than somebody's mother, but she can't know the Sugar bit of my coming life.

The cosmetics bill was just under two hundred and fifty pounds. Christ—I'm going to be clean out of funds before Alain even arrives—after all, my flat isn't even on the market yet…

'I'm leaving you a free sample of the eyelid-strengthening cream', Georgina says before she leaves.

Is he Gay?
—why does he stay away?

∞ 3 ∞

Everyone has a friend who's there to remind them of reality, or, as it usually feels at the time, put them down generally, stop them having any fun and (when in a grumpy mood themselves) rain on their parade to such an extent that they feel like breaking up their umbrella and walking away. 'Oh Scarlett', says my mentor and guide through life's rocky moral paths, when she comes into my flat (and has seen me peering through the spyhole with a pencilled, shadowed and mascara-laden eye), 'What *do* you think you're doing? You don't imagine we're going to have sex with this man, do you? He's probably incapable anyway.'

By this time I'd let Molly in (she suits her name,

she's Irish and has a bob of dark hair she doesn't dye often enough so she appears to have grey handles at the side of her face like a jug), and I admit I was grateful that at least the new occupant of the upstairs flat had been spared from hearing this. He's a banker, part of the new gold-rush of gentrification, and I wouldn't want him to reflect on my preference for impotent men every time he sees me emptying the rubbish bin. 'Of course he can do it', I said, aware I sounded like a ten-year-old, 'I mean, why should he be…?'

Now the thing about Molly is that she knows everything. Even if she doesn't actually know the people involved—and there was no way Molly would have known Alain *and* Claire: she works as a copy editor with a big publishing firm, is always about to be promoted to an editor but never is— even if, as I say, she'd heard of them (extremely unlikely), there would be no connection whatever between her life and the dreamlike existence of Alain and Claire. This time, Molly wasn't going to know best.

'I saw his tiles in *Interiors*', Molly comes up with an unfailing trump. 'Honestly, there isn't a chance…'

'You mean he's gay', I almost shouted, careful to

26

spare the banker as he shuffled around upstairs, getting ready for an evening out. 'What part of pre-history are you living in, for God's sake? He's not an interior decorator…' Here I knew Molly had really got me so I was unwittingly bringing out the old chestnut about interior decoration. For God's sake, indeed.

At the same time, I felt a wave—the first, but there were and doubtless will be many more to come—of total desolation. I'd found all day I couldn't summon up Alain's face (it's a sign you're in love, so I've been told, if you just cannot remember what your inamorato looks like, but at my age it's probably Alzheimer's and nothing premature about it).

I just couldn't help seeing him, faceless though he might be, as he walked to the end of the drive of the perfect house at Bandol and stood waving to me over the banks of lavender that line the road. He was in his romantic-hero outfit, as I like to think of it: open-necked, sea-island cotton, blue shirt, sprayed-on jeans (he's rake-thin, did I say?) and a great, worn-looking, studded, brown leather belt.

'That's why he's so thin', Molly is saying. She has the irritating habit, found often in people you see a lot of, of knowing exactly what you're thinking.

'Because he's ill, he's a big drinker, it's not cancer, wait a minute I'll try and remember what it, the disease is called…'

I confess this came as a shock. Like being in a self-satisfied state after a shopping trip and glowing with joy at your wonderful new purchase and then finding you've been landed with damaged goods.

'Christ, a seriously ill, homeless man is about to throw himself on your mercy', Molly panted when I'd come out with the whole story.

'He'll want to go private—it's three thou a night at the Princess Grace.'

But I wouldn't believe it. Alain is so lively—he may have had a short bout of something or other, and then Claire (but I didn't want to think about this) had cared for him and he was better. He couldn't have come on to me the way he did at Bandol if all the energy had been drained out of him by illness.

Then I thought maybe it was meeting *me* that had suddenly made him well. That's how seriously mad you can be when you're in the first throes of being a Sugar Mummy.

Molly said what I knew she'd say when she'd looked round my ground floor sitting-room and noticed the polished boards and the vases full of

tasteful grasses and the drinks table with the bottle
of tequila and a whole bowl of finest sea salt.

'So where is he?' Molly said.

He Comes at Last

♋ 4 ♋

This is the kind of time when you evaluate yourself (nothing else to do) and find you're badly lacking in pretty well all of the human attributes that can save you when you get to the Pearly Gates (not far off). I'm suffering from sexual frustration when I ought to be collecting for Save the Children. How gross is that? I'm trying to turn Alain into a Romance rather than a simple fuck, so I'm a hypocrite as well.

I've already taken out my calculator and estimated what I can spend on Alain: holidays (luxurious, for the first one at least); outfits (nothing but the best until they wear out, and then it's mail-catalogue lambswool sale sweaters); restaurants (if the evening turns out as I hope, the Kwai Chi in

Fernhead Road will become our local, with all that fresh seafood to assist the libido).

But wait a minute. Alain may have lost his libido altogether if Molly is right—she's sitting opposite me in the basket chair and has been since last night passed without a glimpse of Alain. She came back this morning at dawn, yelling 'let me in' into my intercom so the banker upstairs definitely must think I'm a lesbian.

I'd tell Molly to go, except I feel quite desolate, totting up my sins and misdemeanours. Do men do this? Only Donald Trump, I suspect, but not men who work part-time on rich people's flats like I do and sometimes forget to get in food because it's so stressful when the money runs out. I'm the only self-obsessed sexagenarian (a good word, it cheers me up) that I know and it's only sensible to work out what you can spend on a Sugar Mummy's boy. Sensible because somehow I can see Alain's back-view vanishing down the street if I don't keep an eye on the finance. After all, he's in a desperate situation himself—he doesn't need another casualty of what Molly and I call 'late-Thatcherism-without-hope'.

Still, where the hell is he?

That voice on the phone: it was sweet and soft and I could smell the lavender as he spoke, and at the same time he had a perfectly organised 'everything-is-all-right' tone as if the meeting in the boardroom is the only thing holding him up.

Of course it can't be. I try to imagine him and his wife—poor Claire weeping and saying where are they going to go—and then I try to unimagine it because it's none of my business (so I do have a nice side, really)… and then I think perhaps this is my business after all. Perhaps it's the point.

'Let's go for a walk', I say to Molly, 'and pick up a takeaway from Kwai Chi.' (The fact is that thinking about the sex I never had last night and the scallops and raw tuna and prawns and shellfish has made me hungry.)

So that's why we're two of the most expendable human beings on earth—that is, 'women of a certain age', as we oldies used to be called (what's certain is that most people, and that includes younger women, would gladly administer euthanasia to women heading for the big three-score-and-ten, or over: we just take up too much room on the planet). Think of the Gaga Travel tours, with all those old bags in buses, heading for foreign destinations. We are bags, Molly and me, with a bit of money jangling where the exciting bits used to be.

It's good to be out, though. I look around

fervently, expecting to find signs of the new prosperity that has visited our pocket of north London, but everything is quiet, just as glum as ever, with an underlying menace. You can't relax in these long, drab streets because someone might skip out from an alleyway and mug you to death just for fun.

You honestly can't imagine, behind these net curtains (and the odd upmarket Cath Kidston chintz curtain) that an army of new millionaires is preparing for another day. True, the odd Barbados brochure lies in the gutter—but no limos are collecting club-class airmile holders, no Harrods carrier bags have been placed in the recycling bin.

Whatever do they plan to spend all the money on, once the estate agent's board is taken down and the money rolls in?

'When did he say he was coming?' Molly asks at the bar in the restaurant as we decide on eggs Benedict because it's cheaper—I spent all my money on make-up like a crazy teenager, and Molly isn't one to sock you a meal if you're low in funds.

'Soon', I say, knowing I sound pathetic. 'Soon, he said.'

The silence between us says it all. We walk back along the street of tight-fisted Midases and don't even stop to buy a newspaper at Patel. (What's the point? The civilians and children you saw being murdered on last night's TV won't look any more alive today.)

We stop at the foot of the chipped stone steps leading up to our front door. On the bottom step is the dog shit visited on us daily by the Belgian Shepherd that that daft old man keeps in his flat in what was once the big redbrick Victorian church just behind us. Flats now were a place to worship God in the old days; dogs wouldn't even have been allowed in.

But what right have I to hanker after a church? I'm a woman who's desperate to be taken in adultery (or would that be Alain, as I'm not married?) and I'll be unintentionally chaste for the rest of my life.

'Good Lord', Molly is saying, as I puff up past the poo. 'I call that chutzpah.'

But she sounds admiring, so I know something not so bad has caught Molly's eye. Sure enough, the irresistible form of Alain can be discerned in the low chair by my sitting-room window. He looks weary… wonderfully in need of a bath and a rest…

'That banker upstairs must have let him in', Molly says as I stand gaping on the steps. 'And you must have left the flat door open. Honestly, what's come over you today?'

Come and Go

♋ 5 ♋

Oh God, he really fancies me!

How can I tell? Because of the smile: I have genuinely never seen anything quite so sexy as Alain's smile on that day, which seems a Sleeping Beauty century ago... before it grew so hot you'd offer sex to anyone—in the park, in the ice-cream deli, in the Electric Cinema, where the chairs are so easy you just surrender to lust before the credits roll...

Because the smile hung on a long time, I saw it was a clever way of telling me he loved me, while Molly rattled on about a piece she'd read in the *Daily Mail* about his tiles and his wife's recipes (are you my friend, Molly, or what?) and it looked as if we were having an ordinary conversation with me saying 'mmm… how interesting' and Alain even filling in details of their autumn range, speaking *through* the smile, which I thought was sexier still. *Où sont les neiges d'antan?* I can't remember where those lines from a French poem come from, but even as we sat all three in a sort of enchanted circle, with Molly the elderly chaperone (sorry pal), Alain the suitor and myself—I'm too modest to say it—I knew somehow that I'd never forget that first evening. Just how I'd remember it, I didn't know.

Smiles are free, aren't they? Not that I cared then that Alain hadn't brought so much as a bottle of wine or a present of some kind—after all he was in terrible trouble, what with his housing situation and (presumably) an about-to-be-vacated porcelain factory. He saw me as a saviour—that's what I thought then—and isn't that just what a Sugar Mummy wants to be?

She has to get some kind of payment in return, though, doesn't she? And we all know what that is, to put it crudely. Well, why not? Men have been Sugar Daddies since the Pharaohs; it's our turn now to pay for what we want.

'So where will you re-locate?' Molly is saying to Alain as she swivels round in the low chair and looks at him properly for the first time (the smile, I note with admiration, dwindles gradually and then disappears).

But Alain didn't answer her question, and if I'd been on full alert then I'd have wondered why. After all, he's grown-up, however hard I try to see him as a boy, and he—and, OK, his wife—must have decided where they're going when they have to leave the Bandol Dream House and let the horrible brother-in-law move in. They're hardly going to sleep rough, are they?

Then it occurred to me that that's what Alain looks as if he's been doing. Same blue shirt but distinctly grubby round the cuffs and neck, sprayed-on-jeans replaced by a pair of white trousers that sag promisingly at the crutch but show how painfully thin he is where the belt—a thin strip of plasticised leather this time—holds them up, and shoes you could quite honestly expect to see on a *clochard* dossing down by the metro in Paris.

Where has Alain come from? What happened to Alain?

Of course you'll know by now that I'm a bit of a fantasist when it comes to Alain and Romance. I can't help picturing the terminal battle between him and his wife—all of a week ago to judge by the state of his clothes—and equally I can't resist imagining it's because of me that he's been kicked out of Claire's family home. She's seen that he's fallen madly in love, just as I have. It's one of those great love stories like Paul and Virginie and Héloïse and Abelard (I must be thinking of French examples because Alain is French, I could just as well say Troilus and Cressida), and he has proclaimed his undying devotion to me, despite the rage of the wife he married all those years ago. He wouldn't deny his feelings for me, so she threw him out.

'Alain, would you like a drink?' Molly said. At the same time I could see her looking round the room and spotting an overnight bag, a battered Louis Vuitton, by the door. 'You've had a long journey', she went on, this time sounding just like a nursing Sister who cannot be disobeyed, 'would you like a shower?'

Before I could glower at Molly—how dare she offer my amenities to a stranger, is she suffering from Sugar Mummy syndrome without knowing it?—Alain had risen to his feet and was standing in front of the drinks table, still laden pathetically with the margarita preparations of the night before, including the gardenia I'd spotted at the Notting Hill flower stall on an excursion to buy tequila. I got up quickly—more quickly than I'd been able to recently, I may add, which just shows that abstinence makes the heart grow fonder—and ended up just behind Alain.

I didn't dare touch him, as I tried to explain to Molly later when the full emptiness, nothingness and disappointment of that first evening in London had been reduced from a searing wound to a throbbing which could only be assuaged by discussion.

'But why not?' Molly said. 'He did give off a weird pong, if that's what you mean…'

But I couldn't tell Molly that I loved the slept-in smell of Alain's shirt and the whiff of stale alcohol that hung around the stained white trousers. (How I longed to pull them off him; why the hell was Molly here anyway, it was meant to be our first romantic meeting, Alain's and mine…)

I didn't want to tell Molly, either, that I saw a glass on the table which had clearly been recently used. And I saw the bottle of tequila was half empty. She would have been I-told-you-so about it and I couldn't have stood that. Not then—hardly even now.

'Shall I make you a margarita?' I said in a bright, girlish voice I couldn't believe was actually coming out of me. 'Or would you prefer wine?'

But Alain had clearly had enough already. He swayed slightly on his feet in those diarrhoea-colour cheap shoes and I saw his eyes were like a fruit machine, with his pupils rising slowly and then falling so I began to feel dizzy myself.

No, Alain had to go. He would call tomorrow. Where was he staying? Oh, with a cousin of Claire's, she is married to a famous artist, I can't remember the name, not Damien Hirst but someone like that.

'It won't be too far to walk', Alain said. Claire's cousin lives in Notting Hill.

Molly and I stood by the front door of the flat and pretended not to watch as he ran down the steps and turned left into the grey streets of W9. We said nothing as the vacuum closed round us, and Molly opened a bottle of red wine.

Later, when we'd drunk that and another as well, I saw that Alain had left his Vuitton bag behind and we opened it as if it would somehow provide the answer to the aura of mystery which seemed to hang around him. But there was nothing inside except one poxy tile.

Advice for the Other Woman on Sexual Fantasies

♋ 6 ♋

I am called Scarlett because my mother was reading the interminable Mega-Bore on Christmas Eve (When? We all know it was a long time ago) and, so she's told me about a thousand times, I came out just as the ('I don't know nothin' about birthin') scene began. I am the product—by osmosis, you might say—of the most embarrassing and loathsome sexual coupling in history, Scarlett O'Hara and Rhett Butler.

I was the result of the coy glance the hateful Vivien Leigh threw in Clark Gable's direction when he came in drunk and ready to rape the genteel tart under the sheets (which, as everyone knows, he did). His reward was another coy glance across the breakfast tray on Scarlett's bed.

So, with that monstrous pair as my virtual parents, what would you do in my place when the visitor you thought was coming to make you feel young again turns up a day late, drinks the booze without even pouring you a drink, and shows he's been in trouble by wearing cheap clothes from Primark or, even worse, the property of a recently dead man and acquired under the bridge in Ladbroke Grove?

Would you decide never to see him again? Or just put up with it along with the prospect of a restless night and a counting of hours until it's decent to make a phone call. (When's that? To someone in Alain's condition, it's never the right time to call: mornings he's stuffing down the pills to kill the pain of the hangover; midday, more pills to counter the depression brought on by wasting the morning; afternoon, the vodka, the red wine; evening Irish whiskey—if there's the money to buy it with, Paddy doesn't come cheap in the Harrow Road.) And what if this 'cousin of Claire's' answers the phone? How do you get out of that one? Suppose he was lying and Claire herself is enjoying the amenities of her cousin's posh pad in Notting Hill?

Then the horrible thoughts begin. Is Claire about to throw that coy look at Alain? Did he sober up on the walk back from W9 and give his wife the best time she's had for years—liberated, as she must be, by freedom from running the house in the south of France and from the niggling worries that her brother-in-law is about to throw them out in the street? Has she let herself go for the first time in years?

Advice to would-be Sugar Mums

Don't speculate on the sexual activities of the object of desire. He is either doing what you most dread, or something that wasn't invented when you were young.

Do call him—but only when *you* feel like it—drunk will do, midnight will be fine, on a Sunday morning with the sound of church bells is perfectly OK. It's his fault for not being with you at the time.

Never ever try to contact his current girlfriend, wife, incestuous half-sister or suspect male best friend. He needs time off from the endless stream of gifts, £50 notes, artworks or whatever you're pushing on him. And if he's in the middle of an orgy when you call it's none of your business. Just reflect on why you haven't been invited.

Of course it's easier to give advice than to follow it. Sometimes, as my friend Molly knows well, comparisons are easier to understand than hard-and-fast rules of behaviour. If the difference between what is considered in life or in fiction to be winning or acceptable conduct contrasts badly with the deal you seem to have set up for yourself in real life, then this is the time to think really hard about your relationship. Is it all one way? Are the times you can see yourself as another human being in a couple almost non-existent? If so, aren't you wasting your time as a Sugar Mummy, because this is precisely what it's all about. You're better off joining the Gaga Third Age University *now* and forgetting about the life of the elderly geisha, where service is unpaid and seldom met with a smile.

I shut my eyes—we're back in last night now—and when I open them I see that the giant plasma screen on the wall at the end of my bed (my one great extravagance) is activated. Its pinkish glow makes me feel better and younger, and I prop myself up while still half asleep.

Molly has put on something—a DVD or one of her home-made videos (pray God NOT that)—and it's some time before I see it's *Gone With The Wind,* and I realise (I hate you, Molly) that she's interested in showing me the difference between the kind of gorgeous, wicked time that original Scarlett could have and the miserable fate of her namesake (that's me). Never mind.

I drift off as Scarlett goes into one of her famous tantrums and Rhett showers her with expensive gifts…

Meeting Gloria,
the sugar mummy par excellence

∽ 7 ∽

It turns out the first Scarlett was right—tomorrow *is* another day. In my case, with the sleeplessness and denial of sex, it felt like two days—and that's because, I suppose, my memories are of having sex at night and waking up the next day.

First things first.

I come down from my room with the endless replay of Vivien Leigh and Clark Gable in their primeval relationship (Molly's idea of a joke, but it might have driven me mad) to find my friend sitting in the kitchen with a guest, a woman in what used to be called late middle age, wearing a lot of gold jewellery and a bright floral-patterned dress. I almost groaned aloud, except it would have been rude in front of Molly's guest.

Molly is looking tremendously pleased with herself—that's the first thing I thought—then, dimly (and without even a cup of coffee) I work out why. The story of the uninvited (by me) guest in my kitchen is another of Molly's teases, and boy am I growing tired of them.

So here we have it: this woman of about sixty with hair dyed the bright red you sometimes see in Kilburn High Road and I wonder just how drunk the dyer was when it went on—henna-ed hen-night perhaps?—is sitting right up close to the kitchen table and smiling all over her face (yes, at this hour, if it really is as early as it feels). Her smile is sort of triumphant, as if she's just heard she's been left a packet—and this is in W9 of all places! Maybe, I think in my still groggy way, she's heard how much her flat has been valued at. Perhaps everyone in W9 is smiling like this when they wake up, except for those who never got the sex they were hoping for and found themselves instead watching the millionth replay of *Gone With The Wind*.

'Scarlett, this is Gloria', Molly says. '… You remember… I told you… she's just back from Barbados?'

So what's great about that I am thinking, when

the doorbell goes and Molly bustles out to answer it.

Go ahead, throw parties if you want to, I say to myself a touch viciously, because Molly is a sitting tenant in the basement of a crumbling ex-mansion off Shirland Road and her German landlady is down on her like a ton of bricks if she so much as puts on an old 78 and dances alone up and down the garden.

Before I can go on cursing my best friend under my breath, she's back and there's a young black man following her. OK, call me racist, but I freely admit I thought he'd come to read the gas meter and I pointed to it on the wall. Well, why shouldn't I think that? I'm made to feel like Alf Garnett in the replay of *Till Death Do Us Part*, though, since it's clear what I'm doing, and while I'm glowering at Molly across the kitchen she's doing the introductions at the same time, which makes it doubly embarrassing.

'Gloria's husband Wayne', gurgles Molly.

'Yo Scarlett', Wayne booms. 'How ya doin'?'

Of course it became clear (just as I heard to my astonishment the chime of the beaten-up old church clock at the end of Saltram Crescent, as it marked twelve noon) that of course Molly is introducing me to one of my own breed—although I must say Gloria looks considerably happier than I do.

To be charitable to Molly she's trying to show me the dangers of being a Sugar Mummy. But it's hard to see what they are. Wayne appears delighted with his new marital status, and Gloria, shaking her gold bangles like she's a walking bank, beams at him when he joins her at the table.

'We're going to the shops', Gloria announces, 'the new deli on Fernhead Road. Anything I can get you two ladies?'

But both Molly and I are silent, I because I am now cleaned out—I will have to plead at length with the bank to get to the end of the day—let alone the month—and Molly because she is living on her pension and a small editing fee, which means she never has any money at all.

We're sitting there while Gloria gathers up a Planet Organic carrier-bag and another even bigger bag from which the handles of a Mulberry leather bag protrude. Then the telephone rings.

'I'll take it', I say, remembering at last that I can do what I want here. Somehow, Gloria and Wayne and Molly have made me feel a stranger in my own home. 'Yes', I say into the 1970s bakelite receiver, conscious that three pairs of eyes are focused on me—what on earth has Molly been telling them about me?

'It's Alain here', a pleasant but masterly voice comes out to me. 'Did we arrange to have lunch today?'

'Yes, of course we did', I hear myself saying in the same agreeable, orderly tone. 'Let's go to La Speranza in Westbourne Park Road, that OK with you?'

The voice that was Alain said that would be fine.

So it was under the bemused gaze of Molly, Gloria and Wayne that I left the kitchen and set off in the direction of Notting Hill.

Calendar of Love

♋ 8 ♋

This is all a new experience for me. It's funny how one can remember all kinds of practical—and severely boring—things about life as one grows old, but sheer pleasure is not included in the agenda.

I know that I should go to the doctor if I have a sore throat and especially if the glands in my neck are up (it takes ages to learn that when one is young). I know I should keep some stamps and a small amount of money in my bag 'in case' (in case of what I've never discovered).

I should remember to ring sick friends and listen to all the details of what the illness is doing to them, even if it means missing (a) a favourite TV programme or (b) a possible call from someone who wants me to come out for a meal or make a visit to an art gallery, or, better still, the cinema.

Before you become a Sugar Mummy you have to get rid of all this. *You* come first (except for OD, of course, which stands for Object of Desire as well as OverDraft).

It's like learning how to be young and selfish again. And, as you haven't got long, why not go all out to be a granager—a woman without a care in the world except where the new s tights are on sale, and a good knowledge of today's music scene… but there, I'm afraid, I just can't keep up. Maybe being the same age as the Stones makes that OK—yet somehow I know that it doesn't. Ditto Bob Dylan, although that's about where I stop.

Back to Pleasure. It's a hundred years since I went out to lunch with someone I actually fancied and who might, might I repeat—like me enough to suggest another meeting. More SM rules:

Don't plan in advance as if you were going to the Gaga Reading Group or Bingo Over Eighties Club.

If one meeting is all you have, enjoy it.

Live in the present—it's about all you've got anyway.

☙ ☙ ☙ ☙

So here I am, a desperately cheerful, post-menopausal woman leaving the house in W9, with the Sugar Mummy and her young husband still there in the kitchen—laughing and touching and doing all the things I have completely forgotten how to do—and Molly sitting watching them with a sardonic expression, as always. I know all the way down the road that she knows somehow that I am going to meet Alain and everything will go pear-shaped; she's like that, Molly, she always knows best.

I am trying not to think negative thoughts, but by the time the Trellick Tower has sunk before my advancing steps (a visual trick I have never understood but am always surprised by) I am in a state of gloom not experienced since at least last year.

Shop windows and mirrors. Please! The Who's-that-old-woman-it-can't-be-me syndrome.

The man my age (snowy hair, a cane) who carefully swerves to the outside of the pavement and allows me to walk on the inside, reminding me, as if I needed reminding, that women of my generation are supposed to be living in the eighteenth century. Pass the wig and crinoline…

The happy young couple… how good and well-matched lovers at the same time of life appear when you're looking out for Sugar Mummies and their protégés! (Is that the right word: will Alain be my protégé when I can find a way to help him out of his present difficulties?)

By the time I've run through the pleasureless experiences that can happen to the woman of a certain age (that is, should she dare venture out at all), I've crossed the magic borderline between sad but now increasingly valuable W9 and the Hollywood of West London, Notting Hill (no matter that the grey, grim streets of both neighbourhoods seem much the same: Julia Roberts and Hugh Grant trod here and they're actually paved with gold).

La Speranza is only a stone's throw from the bookshop Hugh Grant languidly presides over in the movie. And as a result a lot of tourists come here. How am I supposed to know the latest trendy eateries? I come here *en famille*—that is to say, if my sister-in-law comes up from Gloucestershire with her kids to visit the dentist, we make it a treat afterwards to lunch at La Speranza—how boring is that?

But there he is: Alain, ten times more handsome than Hugh Grant and sitting in the window as if the best table must by rights be his.

Alain in the pale blue shirt last worn in Bandol. Hair washed, dark and slightly fluffy (sweet!) and face bearing no sign of the haggard gauntness etc. demonstrated last night. I notice his hands, smallish and well shaped, as I enter the restaurant (*don't* peer around like an elderly person who has lost their specs in the library: you've seen him already, you goof), because he's smoking (a Gauloise, natch) and a waiter is rushing up with a glass ashtray and he's drinking—yes it must be, it's all cloudy and white—a Pernod.

He sees me. He reacts perfectly. He knows how to look as though he's standing up when you arrive, but he isn't really. He's just so pleased to see you that you think you are both walking on air.

That's when I remember what day it was, that hot and sunny and deluding date in the Calendar of Love. Midsummer's day, that's what.

Enter Stefan,

the Polish Builder

∞ 9 ∞

The trouble with meeting your Object of Desire and finding yourself sitting with him in the perfect restaurant is it's the end of the fairytale. What did Prince Charming and Cinders do when their wedding party was over and they'd made love in the beautiful rose-filled conservatory and toured the royal gardens and waved to the crowd? Get back to work? Try all over again for the video? If they were happy ever after, how did they fill the time? While I'm thinking these (frankly unhelpful) thoughts, Alain is ordering our lunch, and I nod every time he glances across at me with his great dark eyes and seems to be imploring me to agree with every single thing he decides for the rest of my life.

'The Burrata', Alain says. 'Mozzarella from the Abruzzi. Shall we have that? And the Fiore di Zucchini, would that be alright?'

I nod and almost gurgle 'I do' before marrying this man. (It only occurs to me later that he must come to La Speranza pretty often to know their specialities: this Claire's cousin is perhaps the eater of the creamy buffalo cheese from the Abruzzi, Claire's cousin the nibbler of the baby marrow flowers in tempura, which look like a country fête decoration made by witches.) I'm jealous by proxy, and remind myself crossly that I might as well stay jealous of the wife.

Something tells me there are a whole lot of women who have enjoyed eating with Alain—there even seems to be one at the rear of the restaurant, half my age and waving at Alain's back view as if this will make him turn round and remember he's been madly in love with her all his life.

'That's Esther Crane the sculptor', Alain answers my thoughts, and seems to know instinctively who sits behind him (but he was there before me: what's the matter with me?)

While I'm wondering whether or not to admit I've never heard of Esther Crane, someone comes into the restaurant and Alain changes, his face grows noticeably pale and he pulls out the Gauloise packet—his fingers are too delicate to fumble for a cigarette but they almost do. As he lifts the lighter to it, I have to confess I see the slightest tremble as the coarse tobacco makes its first encounter with the flame.

'Scarlett, Stefan', Alain says, inhales and coughs so the introduction seems, literally, to go up in smoke. Then, the cough turning to the laughter which accompanies anything he—or anyone else for that matter—says, the moment is smothered by conviviality, by the friendly greeting of one man to another. 'Stefan Mocny', Alain amends. I wonder for a moment if he has forgotten my name. And to me, with one of those sweet smiles that cancel doubt, 'we do houses… or rather Stefan does the houses and I do the tiles…'

And the laugh, self-deprecating this time, follows. A long twist of dark grey ash droops and falls on to the white linen tablecloth. Alain is rattled—and it's clear he wishes Stefan Mocny would go.

Now here is a rule for apprentice Sugar Mummies who find themselves in similar circumstances, i.e. staring down into the past of the Object of Desire and wanting—so fervently—to help:

Don't try to kid yourself that he wants the
approaching old friend to skedaddle because
he wishes to have you to himself and whisper
sweet nothings in your ear. He can do this
any time (so he believes at least) and there
really is a reason why he doesn't want said old
friend to hang around a minute longer.
Reasons can include: (1) old friend is husband
of the woman he last slept with; (2) old friend
cheated on payments owed to Object etc. and
this is not the time to remind about a debt;
(3), but least likely, old friend might show
keen interest in me and leave Alain alone and
grieving for the Love Affair that Never
Happened. (As I said, not probable.)

This is what Stefan Mocny looked like (he has now,
by the way, pulled out a chair from the empty table
for two next to us. He is ignored by the waiters—is
he a frequent lunch companion of Alain, are they
waiting for Alain to include Stefan in the lunch
order, or what?) Anyway he (Stefan) has a strong
Polish accent, fair, curly hair and an outdoors
complexion so he's a builder alright and he's tall
and burly and looks as if he's used to getting his

way, maybe a kind of blond mafia type.

'The last project of Stefan's is by the canal', Alain says. He's smiling secretly at me as he supplies this clearly boring piece of info and I know somehow that we'll spend our lives—or at least this afternoon—together.

'A *riad* in Kensal Green', Stefan says and this time he's the one to laugh while Alain thanks a waiter bearing the creamy wedge of cheese from the mountains of Italy. 'So where...?' and Stefan turns to me now, twisting his plump, knotty body round a small chair, 'where do you, erm...?'

As I tried to explain to Molly later, I had no idea I was going to come out with this. Words that would change my life and—as I soon realised—would change the perceptions of those around me from a dull woman of a certain age (well OK, it's the least self-loathing description I can come up with today) to interesting property owner, possible speculator, profit-seeking developer. I was transformed and if Alain was looking down at the book of matches he was pulling apart on the tablecloth, it didn't occur to me then to wonder why. All I knew was that he'd gazed down at the floor once before since our meeting in La Speranza, and he'd been staring at my left arm.

(Note to prospective Sugar Mummies: *do not* wear sleeveless tops. However proud you may be of your rejuvenated appearance, the giveaway hag's arm, with its sagging, wrinkled pouches, cannot be disguised.)

But property, I'm beginning to learn, can cover a multitude of sins. 'I live in W9 and today my maisonette goes on the market', I told Stefan Mocny…

Trapped in a Net of Greed

ᦉ 10 ᦉ

The rest of lunch went by in a blur. Waiters brought the crinkly courgette flowers fried in batter, and a plate of a rustic ham approved by Alain was set on the table—but I couldn't honestly say that I ate anything at all. It was more as if the whole world was suddenly determined to eat *me*.

Here was Stefan, pointing across the road: 'The office of Crookstons is bang opposite us, Scarlett!' (Everyone was using my name now, too. I'm used to being a no-name: it's part of being invisible, the fate of all the billions of us over-age women on the planet. We should all be called Pluto, the planet demoted, for its lack of size and importance, to the status of a minor star.)

'I know Martin Crookston very well', Stefan continued, while Alain picked at his prosciutto (even I can recognise that—they sell it in Tesco—but this one is undoubtedly from Castel del Sangri or wherever the head waiter murmured deferentially to Alain). 'We can go and see Martin, and on the way to your house we'll visit the *riad'*, says Stefan, who must have picked up my infatuation—if that is what it is; Molly says it must be the HRT pills which somehow got stuck in my system since I stopped taking them two years back. 'You'll see plenty of Alain's tiles there', he adds with a significant laugh.

Still, it's midsummer day so why shouldn't I indulge myself, grow rich on the proceeds of Saltram Crescent and enjoy having gone up in the world? Even Esther Crane is swivelling round and staring at me with real interest now, as if I'm a rival and not just an older relative Alain is giving lunch to before it's time to board the coach home. And—glory on glory—I catch sight of my reflection in the mirror above the banquette and hardly recognise it at first. I look much younger—I definitely do! Maybe it's the Pinot Grigio—yes, they sell it here too—maybe it's the trancelike state the presence of Alain induces in me (he's drinking a red wine that lends him that little bit of extra colour he needs. Oh aren't we both beautiful!).

As well as catching the eye of other lunchers at La Speranza, it seems to be much easier to hear what they're saying, too. I'm floating (OK I was drunk, but I'm trying to recapture the feeling) and as I hover above the two ladies at the table by the door I hear one say to the other, 'Well, at least none of my children is divorced.' I see her fellow-luncher wince, and I think to myself—in my moment of triumph at having just what I want, if only for an hour, and what I want is to be a person again—I think how awful for the two ladies that all they have left is the point-scoring, the bitching and all the long days and nights when no one wants to take you out, and you hate your friends and your husband if you have one—

'Scarlett', Stefan is saying, 'would you like to go now?' And I look round the restaurant and see at least four more young men all standing by Stefan, whom he introduces as assistants and builders, and I begin to realise something dimly, perhaps I'd had too much of the Pinot Grigio, but it seems we're all in business now, and I haven't even crossed the road to Crookstons or told Molly my plan to put the flat on the market. She'll be quite hurt when I tell her tonight…

Emma Tennant

'I'll call you later', Alain says to me when the bill
has been produced out of nowhere and my card has
been pushed into the machine that half-eats it and
holds on tight until I remember the PIN number
and too late wonder why they've taken such a big
tip.

'You'll call me?' I say, knowing I sound like a
fifteen-year-old. 'When?'

This wasn't how it was meant to go, not at all, not
at all. The long, exciting, wonderful afternoon has
disappeared, sacrificed to property.

'I've seen the tiles', Alain laughs, but he doesn't
answer my question so he may not ring at all.

I'm mortified; I can think of no other word for it.
Hadn't Alain said he was going to show me his tiles
for my next project—has he discovered there is no
'mansion in Holland Park' and that my life is as
rickety and uncertain as his? Is it not worth his
while to spend time with me in the office of
Crookstons, a waste of his talent to look round the
flats I shall exchange mine for? Unless…

My head is spinning by the time I cross
Westbourne Park Road in the company of Stefan
Mocny and his four employees and enter the
definitely not air-conditioned offices of Martin
Crookston. But the thought remains and solidifies as

70

the appointment is made. ('Martin' is red-tied, rosy-cheeked, genial and strangely absent, unable to recall what he has just arranged only seconds earlier.)

'Four fifteen', I say for the fifth time as the heart-breaking sight of Alain walking slowly towards Notting Hill fades as he rounds a corner by Elgin Crescent. Worse still, a Citroën with Esther Crane at the wheel slows, enters the crescent and stops to give him a lift to Claire's cousin's house. Well, they're all artists together, aren't they? I could die.

'Yes, four fifteen', Martin finally manages.

Of Stefan Mocny's *riad* I remember little. An ordinary Victorian terrace house had been opened up on a street overlooking the canal. Stefan spoke of a learning curve and the need to throw 'a further hundred' at it. A fountain tinkled in the atrium. The tiles looked like—well—Moroccan tiles. Are we both phoneys, Alain and I? Or is my new plan the only way I can count on seeing him again?

Action!

☞ 11 ☜

What happened today makes me think of May, who brought me up because my mother was driving ambulances in the war—that was how the story went anyway. May's sayings stay with me and pop up when a real bastard of a day comes heaving over the horizon: 'It never rains but it pours', 'turning up like a bad penny', 'give him an inch and he'll take a mile' and about a hundred others that are really boring but always spot on, in an irritating way.

Well, 'no use crying over spilt milk' is the first that comes to mind just now, and I can hear May's voice as she says it, when surveying, from her chair in Heaven, the way my lunch ended. (Is Alain no more than a puddle of spilt milk? The idea cheers me up, but not for long. Who wants to place their love and affection in the ingredients of a blancmange?)

Then there's 'make your bed and you'll have to lie on it'—something like that, anyway, and I can remember May with pursed lips telling me it was I who was responsible for my decisions—not her, not God, just me. And it was a saying I particularly hated because it left you so alone in the universe and as uncomfortable as this horrible bed was going to make you feel. The words came to mind because— typically enough—I'd no sooner returned from inspecting Stefan's *riad* than the bell went, Martin from Crookstons was on the doorstep, and thundering footsteps on the stairs showed only too clearly that Gloria and Wayne had spent a more profitable lunch hour than I had, and in my bedroom too. (No, they hadn't made the bed either.)

Rules for a Sugar Mummy (would-be) in reacting to the Real Thing:

Don't show annoyance at the fact you have
just shelled out for what appears to have
been the most pricey mozzarella in Italy,
while Real Sugar Mummy has swooned in
the arms of her young husband. Your outlay

(no pun intended) can only diminish, as you keep a sharp eye on costs, while Real S M will be faced with high expenses and a strong sense of disappointment if she cuts down late in the day.

On no account try to change your Look and imitate the Real S M, as you probably have a completely different figure, complexion etc. and would not 'for love or money' (May again) be able to find an Object of Desire at all. Remember the thwarted Sugar Mummies in the park with their recalcitrant ducks? You'll be one of them —or, to carry the nursery imagery a bit further, you'd be a Princess whose Frog would never, ever turn into a Prince.

So here I am, leading a huge retinue of men up the stairs of my dingy maisonette in W9. A few months back, no estate agent would condescend to stay more than two minutes in the place I had made my home. Now, the bumpy, battered walls are made of gold, the creaking banister is 'oak-lined' and the grubby kitchen is 'an opportunity for renovation'. My bedroom will be described as 'en suite, overlooking the green trees (and dog shit, I might add) of Palmer's Park'. We all look away from the rumpled bed as we crowd in—that is, Martin Crookston, Stefan and his assistant Bill (who looks like a Hitler youth commandant) as well as two other men (one short and same size all the way up, from feet to bald pink head, resembles a walking penis, who is an architect working for Stefan; the other is a builder with cleavage, who stoops over and shows his bum at every possible opportunity).

Martin, who can barely squeeze into the testosterone-filled space (but I'm not interested, I've been ditched by Alain the Mysterious Sexless Wonder), is paying me compliments as if I've done up the Alhambra and am giving him first whack at selling it on a commission of ten percent. 'I've some people who would like to come round tonight', announces Martin. 'Six-thirty OK, Scarlett?'

'Fine', I say. After all, the sooner the better, if I'm going to get my plan off the ground.

'The asking price', Martin begins. I notice that all the men fall silent at this and I wait, as they evidently do, in a state of barely controlled tension. Stefan flicks and unflicks a posh-looking fountain pen; Penis starts some wild electronic measuring of ceiling and window frames; Bill stares fixedly with his Luftwaffe-blue eyes out of the window at the dismal little park.

'Seven hundred and fifty thousand', Martin intones.

Good God, the price has gone up by a quarter of a million pounds since last night!

Stefan and his party are visibly relaxing.

Then a head comes round the door ('it never rains but it pours') and a tall, slim figure in shorts and an expensive shirt edges in a few inches. 'Excuse me…' and he looks at Martin Crookston in the kind of familiar way Englishmen reserve for sodomy or property, 'I'm Nyan', this fabulous figure announces. 'I hope I am not too late to say that I wish to make an offer on this flat.'

Prices Are Rising

❧ 12 ❧

If you get an offer like mine on your previously almost unsaleable flat, you find you're a Sugar Mummy all at once to any man who happens to be around at the time.

Stefan Mocny stared at me as if I'd just breast-fed him and he still wanted more. Bill from Nazi Youth stood to attention like a son who's been sent away to school too young and sees his mother as a wing-commander in charge of his penalties and rewards for the rest of his life. Penis and Bum came up close so I had to edge away from them to the door, but there, more seriously demanding than any of the above, were Martin from Crookstons and 'Nyan' whom I saw, now the setting sun had finally gone off the much-vaunted park, was about seven feet tall and had red hair and a ghostly white skin. He must be the banker upstairs.

Well I didn't have time to wonder what this exotic albino millionaire must be wondering about me. Had he heard me calling Alain's name, to see if the Jane Eyre test works—remember: 'Jane! Jane! Jane!' which the poor governess hears when she's about to give up and go and live as a missionary in India, and her reply, called back across the empty moor to Mr Rochester: 'I come' (could this have been misinterpreted by the banker as a wanker's cry?).

Martin suddenly stepped forward and pulled me out through the door onto the landing. Despite a hasty shuffle from the men now trapped in my bedroom, we were now alone on the landing together, Martin from Crookstons and I.

'Mr Nyan has made an offer for your maisonette here at Saltram Crescent', intones Martin—as if this was just one of my properties, but I suppose he deals frequently with people blessed with what is known as a portfolio: a large number of flats and houses all meant to go up, and soon discarded if they go down, a sort of bi-polar investment strategy.

I can't have understood how precious time is to those who, like Martin, aim to sell as many places as possible in the manic phase and stick out the depression in a sun-filled hideaway, because I'm told again, quite angrily. As Martin speaks, the door bursts open and Stefan Mocny appears, Penis and Bum behind him and no sign of Nyan (I can't help indulging the paranoid thought that he's going through my papers, to see what I pay for insurance or, worst of all, how much the flat cost me all of six years ago).

'Seven hundred and ninety-nine thousand, nine hundred and ninety-nine', Martin snaps for the third time. Then he turns menacingly towards me and says '*a very* good offer', as if I've been let off a jail sentence and told I'm going on a free holiday instead.

'Scarlett!' In comes Stefan, just seconds before the looming figure of Nyan collides in the doorway with Rudolf Hess on parole, i.e. Stefan's assistant Bill. I can't help wondering how Bill's mother—or grandmother, it must have been; it's difficult to get the generations right as you grow old—could have found a German to give her a baby, unless of course she'd been a spy...

That's the trouble with me. I can't help day-dreaming at all the most important points in life— like going out with someone you might, just might, like. Or hearing about a gigantic offer on your flat, one that can change your life forever. Maybe I'm in shock… that's what this odd, fuzzy feeling must be.

Through all the fog I can see, however, that Stefan is now standing closer to Martin than a few seconds ago. He's totting up the price of the house when it's a 'family house' (although few families would be able to afford it) and I even hear him say to Martin that he 'could make something of this'. It's become clear by the way Martin nods and pretends to consider this suggestion from Stefan that they know each other well already.

A silence falls. Nyan has elbowed aside Penis and Bum (survival of the fittest I suppose) and even blue-eyed Bill finds himself at the back of the queue.

Panic. What the hell am I meant to do?

Of course I know what they want me to do. If I say 'yes', Stefan will make a mint by transforming poor old Saltram Crescent into a cross between a Dominican monastery, a mosque and a rajah's palace. Employment, obviously, for Stefan's workforce—perhaps unsurprisingly there have been no commissions since the *riad*. Alain had told me that, laughing, back in La Speranza (self-deprecating of course); he meant his tiles had put people off. He even went on to joke that there had been massive complaints to Brent Council from the pebble-dashed dwellers of All Souls Road and Ravensworth Terrace.

So my acceptance would keep a lot of people in work. It's already clear that Martin from Crookstons is going to benefit from this arrangement as well. As for Mr Nyan, his pale eyes would twinkle if they could. 'There's a real shortage of family houses in W9', Martin is saying, as I still linger on the landing. 'It's what everyone is looking for.'

Yet I feel a pang. Here is where I thought I might make a go of an Independent Life (don't ask), and it's good to have friends (well, mainly Molly) and the laundrette and the park, even if it sucks—it makes me feel healthy to go round it twice and clock up a few miles.

Aren't you meant to think of things like that when you're selling? What about the human side? Is Money really so ice cold that I have to choose between freezing to death and being rich or actually getting colder as I grow old with not enough to heat my bedsit from a lousy pension?

'I'm sure Alain will want to design tiles especially for this project', Stefan says. (He must have noticed the way I looked at Alain at lunch.) Maybe that helps me come out with my answer.

Before Stefan can go on about a new learning curve—before Nyan can say how many hundreds of thousands need to be 'thrown at' my flat—and, most of all, before I can outline my plan to Alain—I just know I have to have time.

'I'll think about it', I say.

Inbox Empty

❧ 13 ❧

After that offer from the guinea pig on stilts (which is what the banker upstairs Mr Nyan looks like, and now I've thought it I can't get it out of my head. If he tries to come down into my flat again I'll feed him a lettuce) I'm desperate to get all these men out of my private quarters and relax while planning the next move.

It occurs to me as I take my mobile off the charger in the sitting-room that there are certain emotions a Sugar Mummy must never allow herself to suffer from. If she gives in to them she deserves the worst of fates for one of my breed: that is, paying all the bills, giving loads of TLC, at least as much as a house 'in need of total restoration' would require, and receiving nothing in return. Nada. Nought. Ground Zero. And it looks as if that's where I'm going. I've been far too soft and sympathetic and understanding to a goofy wastrel (well, he *is* attractive, even Molly granted that) who wants to have his (undoubtedly hash) cake and eat it; and too stoned to make a pass (for this must account for the odd 'nothing's-going-to-happen' atmosphere around him) unless I'm too old, hag's arm etc. for sex, and in order to tolerate my company at all he has to be drugged to the eyeballs.

This is the clever tactic adopted by those picked out as the darlings of Sugar Mummies: keep them guessing. Are you too disgusting or nearly repulsive—or acceptable in a certain light? Millions of women with creams and lighteners and brown-blotch-on-hands removers spend their money and a large portion of their lives trying to work out which category they belong to.

And I'm one of them. Pathetic, isn't it?

No surprise, then, that Messages on my phone shows Inbox Empty, as always. I have to be the one to make the calls. Why should I? I've had an empty inbox for as long as I can remember, and now I've made a packet (about to anyway) from this dreary piece of real estate people are going to be ringing *me*. But am I really like that? Do I believe that there's no real friendship in the world—that people ring someone simply because they've come into some money? Of course not. Scarlett, this property boom and stupid infatuation are together doing you no good. Sell the flat and give a high percentage of the proceeds to charity. (Ha! Wonder if I'll remember that when the time comes.) Get rid of Alain—there, I've said it! But how?

Rules for turning back from the trainee Sugar Mummy into a decent, respectable older woman whose main treat is Sunday lunch with stressed relatives, admiring their grandchildren, or other blameless activities such as making meatloaf for same stressed relatives (seldom appreciated, unfortunately) or knitting:

> Lose a sense of compassion. If the candidate
> for being a recipient of a Sugar Mummy's
> love and affection has been thrown out of his
> home by parents or girlfriend it is *not* up to
> you to provide somewhere for him to live.
> Nor should you throw away your pension (or
> proceeds from a hefty property sale) on
> private medicine. If he dies while waiting for

an NHS appointment/operation, it is *not* your fault.

Throw away the trappings of Vanity: the Manolo shoes, the Mulberry bag, the Burberry anything. Ditto the eye shadow, the crate fillers, the bag-under-the-eyes concealers—let these be the only bags you possess (apart from the endless carrier bags, which old women can't bring themselves to throw away).

You don't need a mobile phone. The temptation to ring a possible Object of Desire can be great, and as you are becoming increasingly blind and deaf you will be inclined to sit on the very number you pretended to yourself had been erased from Memory, causing upset and embarrassment, or, worse, a resumption of the relationship, to encourage a now (wisely) jettisoned candidate to start calling you from distant resorts in order to tempt you to go out for a stint as Sugar-Mummy-in-the-Sun.

♋   ♋   ♋   ♋

So what did I do?

Just as you might imagine. Before Molly had a chance to come round and hear the extraordinary events of the day, I:

Selected the Emma Hope sandals with lace bands and wedges.

Put on my gold hoop ear-rings (drew blood as I had forgotten that my left ear hadn't taken kindly to being pierced centuries ago and had closed up).

Put on three dresses in succession and ended up with black Ghost trousers and long, beaded top (vintage, Portobello Market).

Tied up hair (dirty, no time to wash) with Sonia Rykiel scarf bought at Agnes B.

Loaded on enough rings to knock out a mugger: antique silver, Peruvian crystal, sham amethyst, memorial Victorian ring with name 'Alice Turner' inscribed in gold on black background (don't know who she was, bought in Chelsea Antiques Market, but

Alice you're going to see something tonight if
you're still hanging around somewhere),
eyeliner, Touche Eclat, eye shadow in
turquoise and dusty pink wrinkle remover.

You might say that all granny left out was her
glass eye. But I don't care. I'm going to find Alain in
the house in Notting Hill.

Art for
Desperate Housewives

∽ 14 ∾

Dawson Place is one of those neighbourhoods it's too posh to call it a street—with long, low houses painted a glistening white, *Desperate Housewives* gardens and the occasional strolling security guard, Alsatian and all, where you feel you're going to meet David Lynch (*Twin Peaks*) when the female residents of this Hollywood on Notting Hill district emerge with pets and Upper Gold credit cards to go shopping—or at the very least you'll bump into Pedro Almodóvar, ready to film your nervous breakdown.

What the hell am I doing here? Up in W9 I could be Anne Bancroft—music-loving and with a hint of an intellectual inner life—and Alain, hard to get away with but just possible I suppose, could be the eager young graduate Dustin Hoffman.

Here, you've had to have seriously made it. Stopping outside the most likely house (well, the tile Alain had brought to my flat in his battered Vuitton bag had an address scrawled on the back, so it must be here), it's possible to witness the rewards for an artist in the Saatchi bracket even if it means peering through the Banham gates on the windows to glimpse the Art inside.

Wow! The sheer size of the plaster sculpted baby on view in the window of the raised ground floor! Truculent expression, huge head, mouth like a cavern caught in mid-bellow—who would want that? Don't call me a philistine, I love Rothko and I put my name down for an Ellsworth Kelly at the Serpentine Gallery, but the edition of 'Red Curve' ran out before my name was reached. It would have looked good in a flat I was doing in Fulham (but maybe that's a bit of a put-down, Kelly is now too accessible).

No, I love Art… but the equally huge, purposely smudged acrylic of the Queen dressed up for a glitzy seaside trip, purple-frosted Dame Edna shades and all—I mean, what's the point? Until you see a tiny Polaroid of Princess Di stuck on the side of the sunglasses and a tear painted on the powdered cheek of the queen—well, again, what's the point? Then there are the fish tanks and what look like dead dogs (neighbourhood pets?) floating inside... Where's the space for the people here to sit and enjoy themselves?

While I'm standing on the pavement and feeling like a pickled shark in formaldehyde, some movement down in the basement of Claire's cousin's mansion becomes apparent.

I lean over the railings and stare down. A man is walking around a small room which is the antithesis of the showy art gallery above. If it's Alain, I say aloud, if it's Alain I can suggest a drink somewhere (not here certainly) and put my new plan to him. Then we can go on somewhere for dinner—I'll rent a car and we can drive out to the country, it's midsummer after all.

Such are the mad meanderings of a Sugar Mummy with myopia. Because the man in the basement could never be Alain. Short, stocky, almost bald, the only similarity lies in the fact that the stranger wears a pale blue shirt. And on closer inspection the shirt proves to be a mail-order number, not what Alain would wear at all. Then I nearly plunge to my death over the railings, which I grasp hard before realising they've recently been painted, and drawing my hands across the front of my pretty vintage top I now see I've become an artwork myself, a striped, demented woman all dressed up and nowhere to go. Damn Alain (I can't help blaming him for this) and—why not throw her in for the sake of it—damn Claire's cousin, whoever and wherever she may be.

My Emma Hopes were hurting badly by the time I managed to find my way out of Dawson Place and I waited twenty minutes for a 23 bus to get me back to W9. Yes, everyone stared and some laughed outright. I must have looked like an escaped prisoner with bars painted across my chest! 'That'll teach you'—one of May's favourite sayings, comes to mind. But I've Molly to contend with yet.

☞   ☞   ☞   ☞

It was worse than I thought—much, much worse.

Molly was there alright, waving to me like a lunatic from the ground floor sitting-room window of my flat. What's the matter, can't she see I'm in pain? Then, tears nearly coming—the real thing—and quite unlike that foolish painting of the Queen's crocodile tear as it stood poised to run down the royal cheek, I begin to grow properly afraid. What's happened? Is there a fire? Christ, did I pay the insurance? Is this seven hundred thousand, nine hundred and ninety-nine pounds going up in smoke? God, the sheer irony of it when I was trying to off-load some of it on to a man who never rings me, doesn't care… Well, too late now, my house has burnt down, 'ladybird ladybird go away home, your house is on fire and your loved ones have gone.'

Except they haven't. They've come back! Oh God, now of all times while I stand on the pavement a demented figure with black paint on my boobs and streaks across my face where I've tried to wipe away my own distinctly real tears.

'Scarlett!'

Yes, that's him. To Molly he's worse news than a major conflagration in uninsured premises. That's what she was trying to warn me about: as May would put it, the one who turns up like a bad penny. Howie. My ex.

'You're looking lovely tonight', Howie says when I've staggered up the front steps and he's striding down towards me as if he owned the place. 'Shall we have a drink?'

An Ex

— does he want sex?

❦ 15 ❦

Howie, as you may have gathered, is the very last person I want to see right now. But once a bad penny rolls in, it's very hard to get rid of—and usually it's only come in the first place because there might be other pennies it can tot up with, i.e. some rich young girl, recent widow or divorcée (Howie thinks in old-fashioned terms) or outcast heiress in need of a cause.

The trouble for Howie these days is there just aren't any causes left. But for younger readers of my *Confessions,* let an old woman explain just what a Cause used to be and why every self-respecting girl had to have one or, better still, be teamed up with a Leader of a Cause.

Emma Tennant

In those distant days when Howie was prowling Dingwalls at Camden Lock for directionless Big Spenders whose daddies couldn't wait to get them out of the house, there was an electrifyingly large selection of initials to choose from. Lefties could be Workers Socialist Party (WSP) or Workers Revolutionary Party (WRP) or Trots (Trotskyists) or affiliated to the NLR (*New Left Review*). Girls and women, once the Real 1960s began (commencing 1967 with colour TV and violence in Vietnam on the screen) could join Women's Lib. Even if the New Left was the only New Thing Left for these ex-debutantes and Benenden girls (a posh boarding school), they would not be allowed to join it themselves: they needed a male working-class hero.

Howie was in his element in those days. He stood next to Tariq Ali in the Grosvenor Square riots, he got fired on and squirted with CS gas in the Paris '68 Evènements, and he married in rapid succession a Vanderbilt, a daughter of Dow Jones Financial Index, an English Rothschild followed by a French one. (Don't ask why he married me: I think he'd come to realise that the rich had tumbled to the concept of the Pre-Nup early, and he invariably found himself worse off post separation or divorce than he had been before marrying.) On one occasion, as a mutual ex-friend reported, Howie was able only to afford a stifling walk-up in Harlem and was mugged on the way to the pawnbroker with his one relic of the union, a silver picnic set. (Howie was, like many of the followers of Karl Marx, extremely fond of pretty things, and losing the goblets, fish knives etc. from this relic of early American super-wealth must have pained him considerably.)

So at least, I believe his thinking must have gone, here was a female (that's me) who can type, run a humble business (I co-owned a lease on a small interior decoration shop at the bad end of Fulham Road in those far-off days); I could look after Howie, maybe even take him down to my parents' cottage in Hampshire for fresh air and a reminder of what it is to be English, because for Howie the Hamptons, Martha's Vineyard, Cap d'Ail and huge ranches in Mexico and Spain were all he'd seen for years.

It didn't last. Howie turned out to be a bourgeois at heart. Along with the fearless feminist Molly (how things change! Now instead of marching or throwing eggs at the Miss World competition, she sits at home proofreading and endlessly editing a sequel to *Gone With The Wind,* which has been commissioned but can never be got right), I had taken on pretty well every cause except the BNP, even Oswald Mosley's black shirts in old photos never turned me on. I was too Left for Howie—and I soon discovered I didn't much like him anyway.

So here he is. It's the first time he's visited my flat, as we'd divorced a good few years before I moved here. Sometimes he'd ring from the US—he lived in a caravan in southern California since the last rupture from the ruthless daughter of an even more ruthless Russian oligarch—and he'd sound wistful, saying he'd come round 'next time I'm over'. To my great relief he never did—and I think it was the neighbourhood that put him off: like many ex-pats he sees London in terms of Princess Diana's funeral route, gentlemen's clubs, Green Park, the City and the Savoy. W9 must have seemed impossibly far out, to Howie—but not in the hippie sense of the word, more that of the Edwardian snob.

Now I'm following Howie into the sitting-room, where the state of the ashtray (shame on you Molly) and the drinks tray bear all the signs of a long chat between my ex and Molly. Christ, I know what they must have been talking about, and now I know why Howie finally got himself north of Notting Hill.

Of course! Even an Eskimo marooned on a piece

of melting ice in the Arctic would have heard by now of London's crazy housing boom, of the City bonuses fuelling the buying of any old dump for squillions...

Molly, I say to myself, is my best friend, who has always liked to hear about Howie: when she's not drooling over Rhett and Scarlett there's nothing she enjoys more than to go down Memory Lane with another Old Leftie and talk about when Lefties were New. Now, the only two ideologies in existence, as Howie would gleefully misquote the great Marx, are property and sex).

The next thought that comes to me is oh God, not that... no... I'm the heiress now. He's come to propose remarriage. Howie always considered any wife of his a wife for life—he could have founded the SM (Socialist Mormon) party...

Molly, how could you have done this to me?

As I glare at Molly, seen now walking unsteadily back into my sitting-room, Howie comes up close, nudges me and winks. 'How about a little get-together upstairs?' he says. To my horror I see his trousers bulging and I think if that's a gun I'd like to shoot you with it. 'I'd like a bath first', Howie announces.

'By the way', Molly chips in as she finally reaches

the drinks tray and pours a gin, 'Alain rang. Just after you went out. He didn't leave a message…'

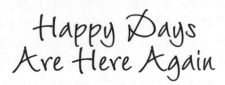

Happy Days Are Here Again

∽ 16 ∾

I suppose the first time I really started to hate my flat was that evening when I wanted so desperately to call Alain and there was nowhere I could be unheard—or not followed, for that matter—with Howie, bath towel round his waist, resembling a retired boxer, going up and down the stairs in search of me, and Molly with her legs stretched out around her on the sitting-room sofa, getting up at brief intervals and shuffling round looking for me—and, yes, Gloria sans Caribbean husband crying noisily in the downstairs loo.

Oh God, there's nothing worse than waiting for a phone call from someone you want more than anything to be in touch with—and finding you're just the same inside as you were a whole half century ago, when you waited and waited for Sam from your local comp to ring, and he didn't, he didn't.

Isn't there a newly invented mobile which would take pity on Sugar Mummies and whisper an address or email address or a phone or fax number? There are enough modes of communication, but the vanishing Object of Desire—'he left no message'—is worse than a ghost: he's a reminder of all the thousands of times you weren't rung back and stayed a victim of short-memoried relatives (I think it was him) or spiteful friends—perhaps Molly falls into this category.

Anyway, I begin to sympathise with Queen Elizabeth the First, who couldn't let herself go in case the man she wanted took advantage of her. Bess had to keep her mind firmly on her status, her wealth, the politics of war and all that. There just wasn't time to sit by a fire in Hampton Court or Greenwich or wherever and wait for a messenger to ride up with a letter in a cleft stick. If she let go for one nanosecond, she'd find herself in the Tower and all her houses taken by one family member or another. If she ever did get free, she'd have lost her homes by the time she was out.

This isn't going to happen to me. Howie, playing

Essex to my Elizabeth, has now changed into a strange blue suit (he must have brought it, banking on staying here, chillingly assuming, as most men of his generation do, that an ex-wife is always up for it and living in my flat was a cert), and he bursts into the kitchen, where I'm on the last digit of Alain's mobile number.

'We could go down to Notting Hill for dinner', Howie says. The bravery involved in risking W9 cuisine is obviously too great to contemplate.

'I've just come back from Notting Hill', I say wearily. 'Thanks all the same.' I try to calculate how great Howie's profit would be if, as he clearly hopes, the dinner ended with an accepted proposal and the ensuing divorce granted him half of my flat: something in the region of three hundred and ninety-nine thousand nine hundred and forty-nine pounds, after subtracting £100 for lobster and champagne at La Speranza. Worth a try, Howie.

'Maybe something local', he hazards, probably regretting that his need for a bath was greater than his desire for a fuck, with the promise of alimony later.

Howie goes into the sitting-room at last and I hear a conversation starting up with Molly. (He's anxious, I can tell: he'll want to know if there's 'someone else'.)

Well, only in my head I say silently and despondently to myself. And, Molly, I'll kick you if you start talking to Howie about Alain. I can see the two Old Lefties sniggering together when she explains the grand villa in the south of France—and, revolting reminder of an aristocratic past, the distinctly unproletarian job of producing hand-painted tiles.

My face is suffused with red when the mobile suddenly rings me back, as if of its own volition, and Alain's voice comes pleasantly soft—and masterly at the same time, I might add. (At age thirteen I was the great fan of the romances of Georgette Heyer.) I hardly notice the door of the downstairs loo opening and Gloria emerging into the hall. She's transformed—all lipstick and hair bouffed up so she wouldn't fit into a London cab without squashing the coiffure.

That's all I did register, because Alain is saying he's round the corner and he's borrowed Claire's cousin's car. Claire's cousin has gone away. Shall we go somewhere for dinner?

Now this is where I'm hit by so many conflicting feelings that I feel like a crossroads where, in the old days, jazzmen played as the moon came up and the songs and the lovely whine of the electric guitar filled the night skies…

Dinner out! Yes, I know I'm invited sometimes by the Porters or by the Howells and always at the last minute because no one wants an extra, older woman mucking up their dinner party, possibly making eyes at a married male guest or simply looking so depressing that there's an early leave-taking.

I know all that and have almost stopped going out to dinner altogether. But a car… dinner in a restaurant…

This is when I either end the (possibly) blossoming relationship with Alain by blurting out my plan, or I stay quiet. In the end, I do both and neither. 'I thought you might have come along today', I say. 'I mean, everyone else was here, Stefan Mocny… and… the banker upstairs…'

'Stefan Mocny', says Alain, sounding amused.

'Yes. The banker offered seven hundred thousand and…'

Before I can stumble through the figures I hear a whoop of joy from Alain. I love the sound, it's like a child celebrating good news and for a moment I know the most ecstatic aspect of being a Sugar

Mummy. Alain is so pleased for me: like in a fairy story, the kind wizard upstairs has ensured we'll live happily ever after.

'I'll pick you up in ten minutes', Alain says.

Reasons for a Sugar Mummy to Stay Sweet

❧ 17 ❧

If my flat's been showing all its bad sides—lack of privacy, bad positioning of amenities (why did the 'renovator' of thirty years ago put the kitchen down a short but excruciating flight of steps, which also restricts its size and cuts out any chance of natural light, when opening up the sitting-room and putting an open-plan kitchen at the far end would have been an excellent option? Why does the door of the downstairs loo, which has to open into the hall for reasons of space, inevitably catch anyone walking past? I've had enough whangs right across the chest to jump the queue for an ultrasound. Why does the front door swing open inwards, giving anyone on their way upstairs the privilege of the view of occupant of said loo rising from said loo to wipe 'n' go?)—then it's proving tonight as hard to leave as to have to be stuck in.

It takes me at least seven minutes to discard the paint-ruined dress, go through all my other outfits and end up with the one I picked first, a black linen number at least three years old and giving no hint of expecting an exciting evening. Play it cool, Scarlett, I urge myself as I go down and try to go noiselessly past the sitting-room—but it's hard to be cool when you're in your sixties and people make as much fuss at you going out as they did all those years ago when you had your first date.

'Where are you going?' Howie is the first to demand, unsurprisingly and annoyingly. I see his blue suit had added to the cockiness the ex-husband appears to feel when entering the ex-wife's premises. And it's infuriating, too, that Howie appears to be checking the china cabinet—some of the plates were given on the occasion of our wedding centuries ago, it's true, but this is no time to turn them over and mutter 'Longton Hall' or 'possibly Chelsea'. I could kill Howie.

'Can you give me a lift?' Gloria asks. She's sitting forward on the sofa, and the bouffant hair is half-crushed. I see Howie eyeing the gold coins at her neck and on her bangles and wonder if Gloria would relax her Sugar Mummy preferences if there was nothing else, i.e. only Howie, on offer.

'I'm not going in your direction', I say, as Molly chuckles and goes to look out of the front window. A faint hoot—I can't imagine Alain sounding a noisy horn—shows he's there. He's here! He's outside in a car, waiting for me!

'I don't know what direction you *are* going in', Molly says. She thinks she's being witty and is even glancing at Howie for approval. 'I'm from Bromley', she adds unnecessarily. This statement often activates Old Lefties to compare boring/ deprived/ dangerous origins and leads to contentment. It's better, at least, to be in W9 than wherever they were born or brought up.

'See you later', Howie says as I rush girlishly to the front door. (He's evidently decided against Gloria and her selection of Thalers and Pieces of Eight: the profit on my flat outshines a whole trading post on the Amazon.)

Now I wish I'd remembered Howie's maddening 'see you later' and hadn't just taken it as the expression used for years now by the young and meaning nothing. Calmed by Molly's complicit nod and assuming she would ensure the imminent departure of my ex from *my* flat, I'm suddenly chillingly reminded of my friend Suzanne, whose ex, long a professor of mnemonics in Melbourne, came back last year after being kicked out by his third wife. He was suffering from premature senile dementia, and walked into Suzanne's North Kensington flat with the announcement that this was both morally and actually his home. Suzanne's friends all tried to get him out, but various objects recognisable even after thirty years' absence proved to this learned scholar that by employing ancient Roman methods of memorising places and speeches he had as much right to the Oxford Gardens pad as his long-divorced, first wife. Howie had better not try that on, I think grimly.

But all need not be grim. Here, for Sugar Mummies on the brink of embarking on the career, is a summary of its advantages (providing you have, as I will shortly, loads of cash):

The mundane will vanish from your life once you have picked on the Object of Desire and are determined to pursue him to the (frequently bitter) end. Washing left at the laundrette will remain blissfully forgotten until you or maybe a hireling collects it. The forgetfulness and ensuing irritation at having misplaced (a) specs and (b) address of a doctor for an ill friend will vanish into thin air. You're too engrossed in thinking about the One You Want, to read (specs) or visit the old friend.

You will find an endless source of fascination in tracing the antecedents of the OD—one recipient of a Sugar Mummy's stipend was descended from the family of Virginia Woolf—and although this caused huge boredom at the pub when brought up (again and again), the melting away of an audience was blissfully ignored.

You will find a whole world—that is, the world of younger people—opens up to you and so you buy *Time Out* and watch youthful singers on TV and go to The Nag's Head to see the latest incest melodrama by a twenty-year-old genius, or Glastonbury, where musicians you've never heard of at all play, and you don't even mind when you slip in the mud.

♋ ♋ ♋ ♋

These are just some of the pluses. Of course, Alain isn't really young. I have to pretend he is, or the pleasure of being a Sugar Mummy would evaporate. A girl in her twenties, for instance, would think him an old man. But that goes into the grim category—

and I must say, coming down the steps (all horribly steep in Saltram Crescent, even at a time like this I have to be careful not to fall), Alain in the little red car, which must belong to Claire's cousin and is parked at rather a peculiar angle to the pavement, looks totally irresistible. Everything annoying fades from my mind: Howie, Molly's jokes, Gloria's obvious vulnerability and my casual ignoring of it, even the ruined dress with its unremovable paint stains and all.

Until It All Goes Sour

❧ 18 ❧

When is a scam not a scam? If two people are (apparently) bent on exploiting each other, is the one who walks away with most of the spoils the victor? Or does the loser retain forever the sense of having been an innocent victim, this sense translating into a state of perma-guilt for the winner?

The words moral turpitude come to mind. Not that I feel it at first here at Marga's Bar, not tonight, Midsummer Night, with tables set out by the little garden area with its innocent box hedges and triangular stone raised island, which block out traffic coming into this dainty heart of Notting Hill. There's an air of secrecy and complicity, with the antique lace shop just behind, and a window full of

French casseroles and Vallauris pottery straight from Alain and Claire country—but I don't want to think about that. It's dark, with one fat red candle on each table; for heaven's sake it's a full moon to top it all! This is the time, now or never, for me to outline my plan.

As happens so often when I'm with Alain, however, something both relevant and disturbing comes along. Down the stubby road leading from the posh gardens and stucco houses of the famous crescents come a woman and a man. Behind them, the moon glows ghoulishly in the sky. A Portuguese silver salver in the window of the pot-and-tile shop catches the moon's rays and assumes the proportions of a savage face. I sense a shudder running through me as I see at a distance the female half of this unlikely couple, but I can't say why. They cross the road and stand hesitating on the pavement. And now I take in the full age of the woman, old or even older than old, face obliterated by a net of lines, neck hunched up under the collar of a coat only a very old woman would need to wear on a balmy night like this.

The old woman has a bag—a white paper bag such as old-fashioned sweets, gob-stoppers, bulls' eyes, sherbets used to be placed in—all the old names from childhood come flooding back—and she stands holding the bag up to the young man at her side. She is half his height and peers imploringly at him: won't he take a sweet from a Sugar Granny who just can't hide her devotion and longing (what if he *is* her grandson? It would give Freud a new slant on the Oedipus complex at least). She wants him to love her, and to show that love by leaning down from his immense height and fishing a sweet from the cheap white paper bag.

But he doesn't, he smiles and pats the top of her messy grey hair and takes her arm to guide her down the dangerous, little road leading to Avondale Park and beyond that out of Notting Hill altogether. 'That's you and me', I hear myself saying to Alain. To do him justice, he doesn't even flinch (maybe he's been in a similar scenario before and has calmed the nerves of older women destined to pay for dinner and suddenly feeling their age) and he replies, lightly, 'no, it's not us—we're in property', and looks across the table at me over the grotesque shadow thrown by the candle. I know he waits for me to say what I want to say and he will answer, as in a pre-written and directed script.

'When I sell my flat', I say haltingly—and Alain's face is like stone now, there isn't a way of telling he's even listening—'When I sell, I thought I'd split the sale money in half, invest one half in a buy-to-let and live in a flat, somewhere smaller, on the income the other half provides.'

Alain nods. I wonder if he actually knows what a buy-to-let is. 'I thought', I go on, 'if you look after the renovation of the investment flat…'

I can hear myself grinding to a halt as a picture of a completely tiled flat, a mini-*riad* (why not add the palms?) swims into my mind.

'Will I own some of that flat?' asks Alain.

So there you are. It turned out we both had the same thing in mind. I outlined the risks involved in accepting my proposition—that all the renovation work (including tiling, of course: I've always thought grouting one of its more exhausting aspects) would be done by Alain for no pay. But that on re-sale of the investment property he would receive twenty-five percent of the profits, this is known as Uplift (I'd taken pains to understand all aspects with my accountant).

If, of course, there were no profits, Alain would receive nothing. But the market is going up, isn't it? And surely poor foot-loose Alain would at last be able to place the proverbial foot where it so badly needs to be, on the property ladder.

On my side of the deal, if there's a slump I hang on to the flat and let it, selling when prices rise what is basically a developed property without having had to pay for the renovations. Alain would get nothing.

And I find—as the moon shines imperturbably on and I explain what 'equity' means (the money invested in a property)— that I'm veering away from a percentage of possible profits to handing Alain a slice of equity.

It is, I decide, worth the risk on my part after all.

I mean, suppose Alain and I were to live together in the investment flat and use the other half of the sale proceeds of Saltram Crescent for having a wonderful time…

It was Midsummer Night alright. 'It sounds a good idea', Alain agrees, and who wouldn't think that when handed the value of twenty-five percent of a prime area flat? 'There's Claire', he goes on, 'do you know, we've been together for twenty-four years—imagine, she was thirty-four and I was twenty-four when we met…'

I say nothing, because there really is nothing to say. Am I supposed to house this couple, people I hardly know?

'We'll find a compromise', Alain says, staring past the candle straight into my face.

ဢ   ဢ   ဢ   ဢ

The drive back to W9 was over—so it seemed to me at least—in a second or two, with Alain just as cheerful as he had been at dinner and me trying to fight amazement and disappointment together. What had I done? I didn't want to think about it yet.

But I wasn't surprised to hear Howie's snores when I let myself in (the little red car darted off even before I had clambered painfully up the steps).

Howie was asleep on the sitting-room sofa. Molly's kicked-off Oxfam sandals lay on the floor nearby—but, as I knew, this didn't necessarily mean intimacy had taken place. She and Howie had probably been discussing the huge offer on my flat.

I can trust no one now. Property is death.

Scam
—is he really after my money?

⚛ 19 ⚛

'It's the plot of *The Wings of the Dove.*' Molly lies back on the sofa, sandals still abandoned on the floor, a statement which declares that I, Scarlett, may go out to dinner if I please—but look how it's ended!—and she, happy, I-know-what-age-I-am Molly, will show who's the best one here by enjoying summer nights walking barefoot to her flat in the next street (and probably, not to put too fine a point on it, also turning down a drunken Howie last night). Molly has the advantage of having been wanted and having refused, whereas I—well we don't need to go into that.

'You know', Molly pursues her point. It's obvious I'm depressed and low in self-esteem and this is just the moment to rub in my minimal knowledge of Henry James. I nod, looking blank and mutter something about Helena Bonham Carter in the film—at the time, as it comes back to me, I'd thought the rich heiress should have been murdered for being so genteel, unable to declare her feelings: why should we all wait for her to die of TB?

'You see, Kate Croy was a new type of young woman.' Molly sits forward, eyes shining. Abstinence has made her hair grow blonder, I think nastily, and then wonder if she dyed it when Howie stumbled into W9.

'What was new about Kate Croy?' I say. 'She just wanted to get married, didn't she? And she wanted to be rich. What's new about that?'

'She wanted desperately to get away from her deadly Edwardian aunt's control', enthused Molly. 'She wanted to marry Merton Densher, who edited a radical newspaper…'

All this is coming back to Old Leftie Howie again. 'Where does this become like what's happened to me?' I snap.

'Because when the American heiress Milly Theale turns up', Molly spells out, 'Kate grabs her opportunity. Like a modern girl might. She'll engineer a way to get the American's money.'

'And who's playing the part of Milly Theale?' I enquired. (I loathe and detest the Creative Writing lectures Molly gives.) 'Why the hell should I be interested in *The Wings of the Dove?* What can it have to do with me?'

'You're Milly Theale', my editor friend pounces. Now, as if overcome by a modest self-satisfaction at her superior knowledge of The Master, she reaches for the sandals and slips blotched and swollen feet into them. Then, unable to resist, she glances at me to gauge my reaction.

'Milly Theale? Me?' I've fallen into a trap I know, but what on earth is Molly on about?

Me, Scarlett, ex-wife of a man so poor that my 'pay-out' from the divorce consisted of half the mortgage payments on the horrible Hammersmith flat we had miserably shared. In order to avoid my having to fork out, the flat was sold, the mortgage paid off, and precisely zero funds remained.

Me an heiress. You must be joking.

Then I remembered. I'm worth (on paper, as Stefan Mocny would inevitably term it) no less than three-quarters of a million pounds—with the odd forty-nine thousand, nine hundred etc. etc. to play around with on top of the three quarter mill. To most inhabitants of the Third—and Second and a good few in the First—World I'm a bloody heiress. Now I'm growing a little more interested in how Kate Croy (raven-haired, scheming Helena Bonham Carter) cooked up a plan to get my fortune off me.

'Kate persuaded Merton Densher to go along with the infatuation Milly had for him', Molly says. 'She went on acting as a friend to the rich girl, and encouraged her to believe that Merton returned her love for him. The three of them went to Venice together.'

'Wicked', say I. I'm enjoying myself now. 'And did it work? Did the heiress give all her money to Merton Densher, just like that?' (I couldn't help thinking, I freely admit, that Henry James must have lost his marbles when he wrote this one. I mean, it all sounds too easy, doesn't it?)

'She died', Molly said, and her voice is so serious I can't help thinking these people who devote their lives to literature really do believe the characters they read about exist, don't they?

Something makes me uneasy and I can't say what. I—as Milly Theale—am going to come badly out of this, that's all I know.

'It worked', Molly goes on in her sepulchral way. 'She left all her money to Merton. He and Kate were free to marry…'

'And then something horrible happened to Kate I suppose', I say as lightly as possible. I've been identifying with Kate all along and it's been a shock to find I'm the daughter of a Chicago meat-packer, or whatever old Mr Theale must have been in order to enrich his daughter so splendidly. 'Poor Kate gets a fatal illness next', I hazard.

'No. It's quite simple. She smells a rat—Merton is a bit funny, you know, not as affectionate as she had hoped.' 'So what does she do?'

'She tests him by accusing him of having fallen in love.' 'With Milly?'

'No. It's more subtle than that. With the memory of Milly. And he can't deny it.'

To my horror I see Molly's eyes have filled with tears. Even when replaying *Gone With The Wind* or working on the sequel with the now elderly author, I have never seen Molly cry.

'That's terrible', I say. 'So you mean… if I'm the heiress and Alain is Merton Densher—and if I give him all my money he'll fall for me in the end?'

'Alain and Claire made a plan together', Molly says. 'Alain would go to London to find somewhere or someone—anything to get them housed and more secure in the future—and you just happened to be in the right place at the right time.'

'So he plays along that he's interested in me…'

'Exactly', says Molly, 'and he may be, for all I know. But he and Claire will use you—just as Kate and Merton used Milly Theale.'

'So what do I have to do?' I say, and I know Molly has won hands down on this one and I should have tried harder at Holland Park comp to read Henry James (but it was always *To Kill a Mocking Bird* that we were given. I can't remember anything about that, either).

'You need to die', Molly says. And then, as if we've actually become victims of that silly melodramatic plot, we laugh and laugh and Molly says she's late for the office and I have to go to the laundrette—so, I must believe, life just has to go on.

More
Sugar Mummy Advice

—research the past

❧ 20 ❧

As I've been reminded in the short space of time since suffering the excitement and subsequent disappointment of going out to dinner (Wow! An old colleague, Henrietta Shaw, remarked yesterday when asking me round for a Scrabble evening, only to be told—rather grandly I admit—that I had a dinner date already. 'Wow' was said sarcastically, but there was an unmistakable hint of envy there too) I've been made aware there are questions concerning Alain that urgently need to be answered. Particularly since he's called this morning with all the promptitude of a well-bred chauffeur and asked what time he should come round in the car so we can set off for a viewing of suitable properties. Oh my God, what have I done? How much 'equity' does he think he's getting—and does he even know what equity is? No wonder he's ready to go: my stiff upper lip at his assertion that his wife would live in any property I bought has left him as unworried as can be. Not for the first time I curse my 'good manners' and the restraint imposed on me by some invisible martinet of a mother. (In fact, my own mother was calm and liked a good laugh and a huge gin before supper; where the hell does my good behaviour come from?)

So, for potential Sugar Mummies (those without the self-abandon of, say, Gloria, who cries and throws herself on the sofa or at the feet of her teenage husband, Gloria who has divorced four times and thrown a party to celebrate each time), here is How to Avoid Being Like Me, i.e. giving it all away before you've even got it and suffering Regret:

Find out more about the Object of Your Affections before you proceed. Any murderers, crooks etc. in the family? Any neuroses, well-known to others but not to you, i.e. anal retentiveness (taking your gifts and tidying them away so they can never be seen again, OR changing locks on the door of the apartment you thought you were going to share with him), or binge-spending, using the Sugar Mummy's credit card for pretended dinner *à deux* ingredients (oysters, pheasant etc.—how can you refuse?) and in fact making a beeline for Turnbull & Asser in Jermyn Street and snapping up a dozen fabulously expensive shirts.

Bigamy—or polygamy—a picture rises in the mind of a line of Sugar Mummies, all thinking they are this one's one and only S M, and all wanting a refund on their investment.

Relationship with his real mother. This is crucial. Does he hate her—as so many sons seem to do (at least those of a certain age reared on D H Lawrence and the fearsome influence of F R Leavis). If his mother is alive, does he refuse to talk about her or go and visit her? Do you find Bates Motel flashes occurring frequently when you bring up the subject of maternal relations and he maintains a twitching silence? If so, as soon as you are

established as his next Mummy—well, need I
say more?

These are just some of the risks associated with
jumping into the role too soon. (On the other hand,
if you wait for a relationship to mature before
committing any cash or valuables to a shared scheme
with the Loved One, he will have aged and you will
have lost your love for him.)

All this takes me back to the coffee I allowed
myself with my friend Henrietta before setting off
to discover the hidden bargains of W9. Alain will
pick me up at the Notting Hill Coupole at 12 and
we won't have too long, so I reckon, before his need
for a drink steers us away from whichever
'cheerful' (cheap) or 'well-appointed' (has a
bathroom) flat we are going to inspect. I need
time—God do I need time, more than sex by now,
so I realise—to work out just what I *am* prepared to
spend and how much, if anything, Alain actually
wants from me. I confess I have no problem with
Henrietta seeing Alain when he draws up in the red
car. At our age, her glance at me will say
everything. (Perhaps it will turn to a look of
admiration: the Manolos have magically slimmed
my legs and the new Diane Furstenberg

wraparound has taken about a mile off my hips!)

But things don't work out quite like that. Henrietta is sitting outside La Coupole, puffing a verboten (indoors) cigarette into the Ladbroke Grove traffic fumes. Maybe she's decided that indignitas, hacking to death with a foul cough, is the best way to go, or perhaps her business is doing so badly she can't afford the trip to Switzerland, the loving medical care and the costly final cocktail? Who knows? But I do feel sorry for her—I mean, she looks so *old.*

'He's trying to find somewhere to park', Henrietta says, blowing a blanket of smoke into my face. 'I had to give him three pound coins.'

'Who?' I'm irritated already that a woman I worked with, doing up those horrible little houses in North End Road, and then graduating, thanks to my superior taste, to South Ken and almost up to Holland Park, hasn't noticed my transformation. It must have been maddening to the Devil, I can't help reflecting, when one of his supplicants sold their soul in return for eternal youth and no one commented on how great they now looked.

'Why, Alain of course', Henrietta says while I gaze frostily at her and order a café-au-lait (it is French here; at least the waiters will appreciate

Alain's laid-back Godard-esque manner, shades, shirt and all).

'He had a pretty rocky childhood, poor Alain', Henrietta says with enjoyment; and it comes to me that my List for Potential Sugar Mummies badly needs rewriting. I'd rather *not* be told all about my—well, my what?—my property I was about to say, because I need to know it all myself.

Before Henrietta has time to go on, Alain rounds the corner of Cornwall Crescent and is almost on top of us, while Henrietta is finishing a brief anecdote detailing the sadly impractical tiles from Bandol installed in Eaton Square in the flat of a publishing peer. 'The design simply washed off when the cleaner ran her cloth over the walls. I mean, it just wasn't good enough…'

But now I see that Alain, like some very thin and apparently perma-white-and-exhausted people, is capable of very fast movement indeed. In one minute this skeletal *Bout-de-Souffle* figure (OK, Howie's crowd used to go to the NFT; what a long time ago it seems—and was—and we choked up on Alain Delon and Alphaville and all the rest)—the other Alain, *my* Alain, is standing on the pavement by our table and I can see he's trying to decide whether to sit down or not. There's only a small window now between a viewing with all the possible excitement of an offer (and oh my God I haven't called Crookstons, suppose the offer on my flat has expired and I'm down to what I actually have in the bank, i.e. overdraft £254, owe on credit cards £1,670) but isn't the market still going up and up… Stefan Mocny said I'd get more next week but I might as well stay with Mr Nyan, he's a cash buyer…

'We should go', Alain is saying in a surprisingly grown-up (not a word I've used before) tone of voice. 'We'll be late for Maygrove Road.' And, as Henrietta stares up at him in astonishment—after all, he's the man who couldn't even fix the colours on a tile—he recognises her and gives one of his incredibly sexy smiles and I see her melt, a cliché I know, but you can almost notice her face turn to candle wax and run down the front of her (unbecoming) striped top.

'Hi Alain', says this pretend young girl, and shrugs in a Gallic way so we can all clock her boobs as they peek out from the folds of an unsuitable-for-her-age bra.

'So what are you doing these days?' Alain says. I register the fact I'm glaring at him, just like an exasperated wife who has to stop in the street again and again for her celeb husband to say 'hi' and receive compliments. All this is putting me off the viewing, I can tell you that for sure.

'Maygrove Road?' says Henrietta brightly. 'Is that where people are over-spilling from Queen's Park these days?'

Again, I have reason to admire Alain even though I'm furious with him. He knows not to give away our secret—well, that's how I felt about it— and I still do, ass that I am. 'Our secret' indeed! It's only giving away hard-earned money (as I now see the increase in value on my flat: after all I was struggling to earn a living all the time I've lived there and I've had stress illnesses as a result: I *deserve* the huge sum I'm about to be paid).

So, as I just said, Alain doesn't reply to Henrietta's question and we leave her there, sitting at the table with a blush still on her face and a sagging jaw, and a puzzled waiter, Italian-looking and young, bending over her as if he can't resist staring right down past the Agent Provocateur Spank-me-I'm-a-Naughty-Schoolgirl bra at her old grey tits.

They say you only have to think something bad about a person for exactly the same thing to happen to you.

So here it is. I just never felt in my life anything like the sheer charge, the electrical communication... the sexual chemistry... it's like being on a shared drug and at an opposing voltage so his High meets your Low and you're both floating, diving, soaring...

I can't do better than that. Alain's profile in the little red car is unchanging and we drive along at the speed of old-age pensioners out for a spin in Torquay. I don't think we ever stopped at a red light— but we aren't run into or vice versa, either. We are on another plane: perhaps we have actually become invisible.

Clearly, these are signs a Sugar Mummy should counter with the strictest caution. Sixty-nine Maygrove Road, a house puffed by the agents as 'West Hampstead', a fine family home in need of modernisation, private rear garden' etc. had become Nirvana. Whatever it was like, I would buy it—and for however great a sum was demanded of me.

But first—and this I had ascertained in a phone call earlier to the offices of Hengrove, Layward & Bull and so I knew 69 Maygrove Road to be uninhabited but still furnished—first I would seduce Alain there. On the top floor... it feels more protected and sexy; and we can look out on the private rear garden without anyone seeing us in return.

My sole piece of advice to an aspiring Sugar Mummy in these circumstances is: turn round and go home. And don't throw yourself at someone else out of pure frustration.

Remember that a man who actually believes a relative stranger is happy to give him a sizeable lump of equity in a property in order for him to house himself and his wife is not the most sensitive of mortals. He won't even notice what you're trying to do.

None of which makes any difference to me.

The Property from Hell

❧ 21 ❧

The house in Maygrove Road—well, have you ever been in a place you knew was evil, where there must have been a murder or at least a succession of property deals that were crooked and wrecked people's lives, or maybe just a lot of unhappiness and abuse, that kind of thing?

No. 69 Maygrove Road stank of everything. You wouldn't want to put your bag down in the hall, let alone enjoy sex for the first time with the Object of Desire. In fact, you'd rather enter a nunnery than indulge in carnal romps in this House from Hell, all three floors and a basement too terrifying to try and go down to. Ping! That was the fireplace on the ground floor as we walked past: our mere presence dislodged a fall of soot that would bury Santa Claus. Pong! That was the smell of rotting goldfish from an abandoned tank on the half landing as we went up. Pang! That was what I felt as I climbed and climbed and Igor the estate agent extolled the wonders of the place.

I had a pang because I realised that Alain, with a past lived in Provençal splendour and no notion of the dumps people are forced to buy and 'renovate' these days, must think this is the kind of house I actually want to live in. To him, I'm a Woman Without Qualities, a tasteless commonplace piece of suburban sadness—an interior decorator who has demeaned the glory of his tiles by asking to include one in some ghastly flat I'm doing up, probably in Balham.

To Alain I must be shit.

'Three floors!' Igor is saying; and I clock the fact he's checked out that I'm selling two floors, i.e. my maisonette in W9 and looking to trade down into a bigger place in a less fancy area. 'Loft extension a possibility', Igor wheezes—and it's when I turn a gaze of deadly hatred on him (if they froze me now I'd be the Gorgon, the Medusa with my victims petrified by my glare) that I notice the absence of Alain. He's nowhere to be seen, and my tinny calls, shrunk to a mouse squeak by the infernal vibes of the house, raise no reply at all. (I just hope, for his sake and for his lovely wife's sake, that he hasn't gone down to the cellar, undoubtedly the bourn from which no traveller returns.)

'Roof terrace', pants Igor, opening a window leading out to a collapsed water tank and an area of dented and uneven creosote. 'Conservatory extension may be added from kitchen below…'

I really believe the garden attached to the rear of the house would be enough to give a rational person nightmares for many years. Coils of rope hang from the single tree, suggesting recent hangings (is it an accident that kicked-off shoes and a three-legged chair stand beneath the tree?) while the remains of a dog stick out from a flowerbed.

It was one of those Labrador/ golden retriever/ collie crosses by the look of it that start life in Notting Hill, run north of the bridge on a night when the full moon shows up the train carrying nuclear waste from east to west London, while the property-investing bourgeoisie sleeps happy in the knowledge of today's percentage gain, and ends up (the mongrel, that is) just where the budding capitalists don't want to be—on the wrong side of the tracks.

'There's a lot of interest', Igor says. It's hard at first to believe he means the interest is in the house and not just the interest he imagines to be building up in my bank account. (Of course: he's from Crookstons too—who isn't?—and he knows about my offer. Probably thinks I'll run off to Rio with the cash if he doesn't nail me down in Maygrove Road.)

'I'll think about it', I say, as I reach the hall, with its 'original tiles' (Igor) chipped, stained and with cat poo doing the grouting, if you look closer.

And here is Alain. Someone has left a semi-functioning, brown leather armchair in the bay window, and behind it though the dust and what look like semen stains on the (miraculously unbroken) glass I can see the garage opposite and next to it a brown kind of pebble-dashed building which must provide just about the most horrible view you could find in all of London.

Alain sprawls in the leather chair, a bunch of stuffing protruding just above his ankles, giving him the air of an abandoned scarecrow.

Alain sees me—I suppose he does: he has this weird way of staring at you so at first you're flattered and then you're annoyed and finally worried—and he says nothing at all.

Then it hits me. Alain thinks this shitty house is

where I want to split my famous seven hundred thousand etc. etc. into two dwellings, one for myself and the other for him and his wife. Even if we're out in the street, his lazy-but-defiant pose in the broken chair seems to say, we'd rather *be* in the street than living here. Even if you—that is, me—spend all you've got on it we don't want it. Sorry, this has all been an embarrassing mistake.

I never felt so humiliated, so wretched, so unhappy, so murdered as I did then: all the feelings the house enjoys bringing out in viewers, I daresay.

'I didn't even want to come here', I begin.

Then I see, as a ray of deep yellow, climate-change sunlight comes into the ground-floor space ('double reception, open-plan kitchen', Igor snorts behind me) that there's a good reason for Alain's stillness at 69 Maygrove Road.

He's asleep.

One minute later and we're on the road (he's awake, even quite alert. Pathetically, I'm impressed.)

'Where shall we go?' Alain asks as Igor waves us a miserable goodbye and the little red car heads back to comparative civilisation. 'I need a drink.'

'How about La Speranza?' I have to say.

The Snatch

♋ 22 ♋

So here we are again. Be patient: it won't be for long. But while I wait for Simone to come up with the menu (newly encased in expensive suede: with a regular patron like me, they can afford to splash out), I'm going to give some tips for Sugar Mummies on how to avoid jealousy—or at least not give away the existence of the green-eyed monster just above the Harvey Nicks under-eye bag remover for Old Bags who want to look dewy and young.

Do not stare at the girl (seldom *woman*) who has clearly just become the Object of Desire of your Object of Desire. She will be thrilled to see your obsessive interest in her, and before you can say

Desdemona she'll have dragged the man you call your protégé into the back room (in this case, at La Speranza there is no back room, only a bar and openly visible wood oven and gas hob. But she'll manage somehow: there's always the tiny, all-glass loo where it's hard to differentiate the hand-basin from the WC. But she'll find a way).

This advice, I may say, is hard to follow and I failed dismally. Because (so I believe) you can tell if people have had or want to have sex together by the way their backs and especially their bums hang while their owners are apparently innocently engaged in small talk. A man cocks his bum (so to speak) so it tilts sideways, neither ready to join in sex nor yet sure of further thrusting potential. A woman clenches her buttocks, ready for courtship dance or refusal. A jilted bottom is easy to pick out by its droop and awkward positioning.

And the reason I flipped was because Alain, who had risen (apparently innocently) to go to the toilet at the back of La Speranza, had 'bumped into' (here both bums make a furtive tryst) Esther Crane (who else?) and now stood at the far end of the room with the casual stance of a laid-back man without a thought of sex—while Esther, standing and laughing up at him, was drawing in both front and back bottoms as if she feared she might never breathe again.

Next piece of advice: if you suspect an assignation is being made, *do not try to follow the about-to-be lovers. This will result in humiliation and possibly a traffic accident.*

Well, there was no car crash, but when I saw Alain, as strangely animated now as he had been lethargic on our property-viewing expedition, slip along the far side of the restaurant and (so it seemed) out into the street, I just had to push my way past the ladies discussing the shortcomings of their offspring: 'They never get in touch', 'At least they're not divorcing', 'No what I mean is they never get in touch with *me*', and find out if Esther, by some magic means or another, was joining him out there (after climbing through the loo window perhaps. This brings me to the next tip: if your new rival is slimmer than you, don't try out her escape route. A stuck Sugar Mummy is an unattractive sight).

Yes, they're both there. But not in the street: in the small lobby, where an outdated cigarette machine stands, as décor I suppose, with ancient Marlboro Lights arranged in a dusty parade behind the Perspex screen.

Esther, unseen by me as she made her way

Emma Jennant

through the room, is with Alain and both are
banging the machine and laughing: she must think
it wildly humorous that a man can show himself so
desperate for a fag in this day and age that he'll
attack a piece of dead metal.

'I'm hunting for Gauloises.' Alain has seen me
and immediately both he and Esther re-align their
bums and adopt the posture of the vicar's wife at a
tea party. 'You might get them at Rococo, the
newsagent', Esther says, as if she really wants him to
run down to the corner—and it works, off he goes.

Now just at that moment, as Esther and I in a
confused after-you play make our way into the
restaurant again, a motorbike roars up outside and a
tall, anonymous figure (helmet visor down, black
leather armour all over) pushes his way in. Everyone
looks up. Then the unknown warrior, spurs
brushing the Knightsbridge court shoes of the
lunching ladies, makes for me with huge, leather-
clad fingers as Esther stands back in amazement. He
calls my name, which emerges from beneath his
Iron Cross and beaten silver breastplate as a muffled
roar.

'What?' I struggle feebly as the vast mitts propel
me to the door and past the machine where Alain
had found no satisfaction.

'Hor—', shouts the knight—or denizen of hell. He now holds my arm in a grip that deserves 'vice-like' as a description. Faces peer from La Speranza: 'Whore? Who is this? How dare he?' a passer-by, an elderly man pushing a Zimmer frame, has the courage to call out.

Then I am kidnapped by Stefan Mocny, king of West London Marrakech, his blue-eyed assistant waiting patiently by the kerb. I now see Alain, as if a million miles distant, walking at his normal, lazy pace back towards La Speranza. Then a great, black-gloved hand lifts me on to the pillion seat, the engine gives a shattering screeching roar and we're off, down Ladbroke Grove and under the motorway and over the bridge that crosses the canal.

'Hormead Road', Stefan booms, as I cling desperately to him, his voice muffled by eight layers of protective gear. 'The perfect investment, the house you're gonna wanna buy…'

Organic Cock

♋ 23 ♋

Love is blind, so it's the worst thing that can happen to someone who makes their living from 'seeing' the best way to do up a flat or house, and from a 'vision' of what it'll look like once you've opened it up/ made a new basement floor/ filled a dreary Edwardian nightmare with what agents call 'natural light'.

So it's professional suicide to be blinded like Oedipus by previous sins (in my case trying to buy poor Alain) and finding yourself wandering the deserts of Bad Taste and the pinnacles of kitsch without eyes to guide you. (I can tell Maygrove Road is no good because love needs money and the terrifying squalor and ugliness of this 'fast-improving' part of W9 can never be conquered, even by a Sugar Mummy with pockets deeper than the vaults of the Bank of England.)

But with 29 Hormead Road... here I am thinking, oh well, this is modern, this is smart... and I might as well be fooling myself in the Harrods Furniture Department, somewhere I would of course never go, into buying an imitation Pompadour dressing-table or the like. That's how crazy my unrequited passion has made me. I'll be buying silver fish knives next and getting my crest engraved on them (if I had a crest, that is, but if the nouveau-riches Russes can invent one so can I— how about a sugar bowl with boobs rampant?). Well if you've taken leave of your senses the first thing you need is some degree of respect, a contrast to Molly's brusque remarks and the over-familiar ways of the unbanishable Howie.

Macular degeneration must explain my reaction to what seems to be basement flats on top of one another, identical so you can't tell which floor you're on, which comprise 29 Hormead Road. Floors of imitation pine (now this is something I can spot a mile off). Walls 'dragged' in crude 'Mediterranean-style' blues and ochres. Nylon rush-matting stair carpets. Fake chrome 'steel' worktops that are already dulling, and wood that isn't even MDF, again with an expiry date all over its bulging, giveaway spill by kitchen cabinet door or low-down in casing of Jacuzzi bath. Mock parquet in open-plan etc. etc., colour of an Irish setter's poo. Shades over windows, frail shutters in ill-disguised plastic... outside, a minute patio stuffed with begonias and a solitary pine. Mosaic tiles like a children's cheap colouring book: I had to be glad Alain missed the boat and didn't come up here.

'It's lovely', I say.

'It's what you're looking for', Stefan Mocny says. We're on (I think) the middle floor and as I'm standing by the window I can see the full extent of the modest outlook on offer in this street that's 'on the canal' but isn't: you can't see it from this side of the road although a small gate is visible opposite which opens on to a stretch of brown water (a few inches can be glimpsed). 'Just what you're after. I would have told you about it first except the owner wants instant cash, he wants someone who can free up seven hundred grand by the end of today and I'm showing only the most important clients from Crookstons...'

Just as I'm thinking (1) so Stefan Mocny is in with Crookstons, (2) how on earth does he think I can 'free up' a sum like that? and (3) hey, wait a minute! This place could in fact be a good investment: Top Floor Alain and Claire; Middle Floor rented out; Ground Floor me. Just when the daydream builds I see Claire up there above me going happily about her shopping and pot-throwing while I'm in bed two floors below with Alain, and money pours in from the middle-floor tenants, I realise something funny is going on, i.e. Stefan has come right up close to me. I can smell a kind of exotic patchouli scent on him. Quite honestly, in the murky non-light of the flat, it takes me longer than it normally would—even for someone as out of practice as I am—to see (we're in the kitchen and I thought it was something to do with cooking, an organic ingredient for a tagine perhaps) that what Stefan is holding is his own cock, and he's nuzzling it up against me, muttering about freeing up the money today and the incredible investment this house is, all the way.

If love is blind when it comes to interior decoration, then it's super-myopic when trying to identify the one who is the Object of Desire. As I push away—grazing a buttock on the sharp corner of a tile 'island' (ugh! Tiles painted with bunnies and wizards; maybe this is meant to be the nursery floor)—I see a figure loitering on the far side of the fake mahogany flat door and outlined against 'teak' banisters and a staircase hung with hunting prints and Indian erotic postures (I can't think what else to call them: did they inspire Stefan Mocny into exhibiting himself in this way?) At any rate, temples and naked humans and a couple of nails stuck in the wall without a picture hanging from them suggest a hurried presentation of the property to those able to free up the asking price by 5 pm today.

The figure is Alain. A Gauloise droops from his lip; otherwise he looks as fresh and adorable as a hero in a fairytale, if slightly bemused by the sight of Stefan and myself in the middle kitchen of 29 Hormead Road. I glance sideways rapidly: no sign of the cock, thank God, to make Alain jealous in these surroundings, and after so short an acquaintanceship on my part with Stefan would have been embarrassing, while to witness a total absence of jealousy (as I suspect would have been the case) simply depressing.

'Yo, Alain', Stefan says in his most affable tone. 'This is the property Scarlett here is gonna buy. She can free up the cash now, it's a bargain. Hormead Road is where I'm gonna invest. Tell her she has a great investment opportunity…'

Emma Tennant

Alain walks to the far end of the flat and holds his hand up to his ear, as if a mobile phone conversation with Stefan is taking place. 'I'll put it to her', Alain says into his hand, and he smiles at me. Christ! Don't tell me I just bought 29 Hormead Road!

Kill Myself

how to avoid the end

∾ 24 ∾

Last night was pretty uncomfortable—and not just because the midsummer weather makes you long for anyone but Rhett. Yes, when I got home after my Hormead experience, and spent a lonely evening phoning round (everyone was out, every self-respecting unattached woman or girl was paired off, even the old ones having found an elderly ass to fall in love with, one must imagine). Yes, Molly had put on the *Gone With...* DVD and I half-woke, almost-vomited all night at Clark Gable as he tortured, smarmed over etc. the scheming Vivien Leigh.

So not my type, Gable. Too masculine? Does he seem more disgusting since I was put on Tamoxifen and my female hormones were suppressed? Do I desire Alain because I'm now a homo, a gay man who loves him for his feminine side? Is Alain's apparent passivity feminine, anyway? You can see what kind of night I had. And here I am. I should be sought after by now, after all I'm shortly to be worth seven hundred and ninety-nine thou plus and you'd think the pavement in Saltram Crescent would be as full of toy boys queuing for my favours as the day before Christmas at Hamleys.

Am I to end up in another Henry James novel—that's how Molly would see it, I know—that one they filmed as *The Heiress,* but in fact is called *Washington Square,* a rich old father and the daughter he won't allow to marry the man she loves (because he's a fortune-hunter, natch). The book ends with the spurned lover coming round after yonks away—but our poor little rich girl Catherine just sits there when he knocks at the door and you know she's condemned herself forever to spinster-hood and sadness. Is this what's going to happen to me? Is Alain going to appear in x years' time (Jesus, how old will I be by then!) and I'll just be sitting here, wrinkled as a prune, drinking gin with Molly?

You may ask what Alain was doing last night—and who says he's a fortune-hunter anyway: a slice of real estate offered by a potty old woman (that's me) is likely to be acceptable to most men, especially if they've been told they've got a matter of days in their home and then it's out they go. But I know that doesn't answer the question: I'm here and he's not. If we're going into business together, shouldn't we be discussing the pros and cons of 29 Hormead Road (I'm still drinking the Titania potion on that one, it's the eccentric but just-possible idea of us all sharing—and after all why shouldn't we—that turns me on. It's not as if we're swingers or anything, just that a man who won't shuck off his wife is somehow to be admired and his plans gone along with. Do you agree?

But it's almost impossible to have that kind of conversation with yourself. Even Howie would have been better than no one: he'd have gone into the dialectics of a threesome and he'd have factored in the identical flats at Hormead Road. His long-finished-with personal interest in my fortune, of course, would have resulted in him advising strongly against the arrangement—or the 'compromise', as Alain had called it. Does the word make more sense in this slightly shoddy proposition if it's in French?

Then there's Molly. I knew somehow that she

and Howie had become an item while I was either daydreaming about Alain or out property viewing with him—but it came as a shock around midnight, when I'd been tossing and turning for three hours, to hear the front door opening and shutting again as stealthily as they could make it, a sound which invariably wakes me up.

Then I heard them tiptoeing up the stairs to the spare room—a box-sized, in-need-of-replastering cell I should use as a study but never do—and then, inevitably, I heard the sex begin and I can tell you Molly's effort to moan etc. quietly was the most simply awful thing I have ever heard. At the same time, Vivien Leigh is sitting up in bed and ogling Rhett with her 'I know I've got to fake an orgasm in this scene' look on her face. 'How the hell do I do that?' And quite frankly I could have committed suicide there and then.

What I do in these circumstances is try to think about practical matters—so here, for desperate Sugar Mummies, is my list of How to Avoid Killing Yourself on a Saturday/ Bank Holiday/ Midsummer Night when everyone's unreachable and you've been left alone at home by the man you had offered half your fortune to so he might at least have taken you out to dinner:

Go through your bills and bank statements in your mind. (Yes, so dreadful that stopping makes you grateful to be alive.)

Calculate how much rent you could get in if you don't sell your flat but stay on with a possibly compatible lodger.

Make a mental list of all the things you've forgotten or postponed: (a) filling in the electoral registration form from the town hall; (b) collecting Nectar points for your electricity bill; (c) changing the direct debit on your mortgage payment to the bank account with the smaller overdraft; (d) forwarding the mail addressed to the previous occupant of the flat, still coming sporadically after eight years.

And so on. If you're not asleep yet, I'm surprised. But I just got more and more wakeful, rehearsing my uncertainties—over Alain, over Hormead Road, over his sweet polite smile when he dropped me off here saying Claire's cousin needs the car tonight and they're going together to a friend's private view (hurtful: why not ask me?) My rating must have gone right down—he probably despises Hormead just as much as Maygrove Road. He can't live with me anywhere because of my appalling taste in property.

I should have called Crookstons when I came in, I know. But I've no idea what to say to them. I even don't know if I want to sell my flat at all. (Silence from Mr Nyan upstairs: he's probably gone away, maybe he'll change his mind too and withdraw his offer, which would be a relief, oh for God's sake withdraw it, Mr Nyan.)

So pity me, lying here with my eyes shut against Rhett and Scarlett and my brain swirling. I can't bear it, I can't bear it…

A moth or a beetle (all I need really) flies in through the window and my eyes open. And I see the answer in, of all places, Tara. Scarlett kneels on the ground, pulling up lumps of red Atlanta soil. For her, home and land are everything… she will never let them go. I'll never move from my home, I promise myself, after all.

Who Wants to Be a Millionaire?

— I don't

～ 25 ～

I'm a new woman today. Getting up early is good for you! Growing old is 'comfortable and friendly'—this from a column in *The Times* by agony aunt Virginia Ironside, who celebrates the hanging folds of skin waiting to cascade down her body when she stands on her head doing yoga. At 62, the only relationship she can trust is with her three-year-old grandson—and she's so happy.

Virginia is right. She doesn't have to dress up for anyone; she kicked off the Patrick Coxes ages ago. No Sugar Mummy she—though we can see she's coloured her hair to hide the Salt and Pepper. Why doesn't she go the whole hog and empty the contents of a crisp packet on to her head and be a Vinegar

Aunt? Because I bet she's really longing for an Object of Desire and she hasn't got the bottle to go out and find one.

It's going to take me time to turn into the cosy old woman people expect and seem to want—like grandmothers are OK but don't whatever you do look like my mother. Maybe that's it, the Caribbeans have got it right, with the kids brought up by grannies and their mums out working all day and going off with whoever they fancy at night.

I'll take up Gloria's invitation to St Lucia (she's gone back there to return Wayne to the shack above Soufrières where he used to pick bananas for a living, but now the Americans have ruled the fruit all have to be straight instead of bendy so he's out of a job, which is why he picked up Gloria on the beach in the first place). I'll go there and just be myself, I'll be as old or young as I want.

It takes me some time to realise that I'm just where I was if I don't sell my flat. I may be feeling pure and reborn, someone who doesn't find they have accidentally tempted an indigent tile designer into an immoral and financially disastrous threesome, but where exactly does that leave me? With my bank overdraft and very little work coming in (no one wants antiques these days, it's the age of minimalism and who can survive by selling one ceramic bowl with an apple in it to go on the chrome-and-steel kitchen worktop and possibly a single Shaker chair for the media section of the newly refurbished duplex?

We all have to make sacrifices. After my excruciating night I've lost my paranoia (it comes with giving up a thirst for money, for profit, Boom Disease as I now see it), and a wonderful sense of grace flows through me as I remind myself that (a) Howie can take nothing from me (he took my self-respect and optimism for the future years ago anyway) if I don't sell; (b) no one will try and make me buy Hormead Road if I haven't sold here and am therefore penniless; and (c) Alain will disappear as noiselessly as when he came, on discovering I'm as out of work as he is, have no expectations (and thus no lunches at La Speranza to provide), and that a sandwich—or worse, one of Molly's stews—at Saltram Crescent is no fun at all.

A sense of relief greater than any I've known since spraining my ankle on the last day of summer term at St Winifred's and so being spared the swimming race washes over me again.

I rise, mutter a quiet imprecation at the sound of tramping footsteps on the stairs—but they seem to be going down rather than up so I must be grateful.

I'm a different person today, a woman who accepts her age and will dedicate her life to helping others. (This seems to have slid into the third person: is it because it's a resolution which can't belong to me?)

But maybe I should explain the kind of night I had...

And perhaps that will stop me obsessing about love.

In the words of the great philosopher and psychoanalyst Jacques Lacan, 'Love is giving something you haven't got to someone who doesn't exist.'

I know what he means. Never was the non-existence of Alain more evident than in the long, dark night of the soul, the agony of my time alone with Clark Gable and Vivien Leigh, suffered to the accompaniment of Molly's groans and cries and ending (a new one, this) with what sounded like a huge army of Polish builders arriving at 5.30 a.m. and beginning (so it sounded at least) to tear down the upper part of the house. What did I do to deserve this?

And the answer came cool as one part of Lacan's dictum: You didn't have love, you don't have love and you never had anything to give. Only money and a promise of a property you could never have shared. Lies, lies, lies…

Molly says you never get rid of a Protestant guilt complex—and on top of the Polish yells and shouts, and the sound of sawing wood and doors being kicked in, this was about the last straw. Horrible possibilities suggested themselves: that Mr Nyan, assured by Crookstons of my acceptance of his offer, was rearranging the house to suit his needs (this turned out to be true); and, worse, that my ex, the now snoring and sex-sated Howie, still retained a Power of Attorney enabling him to sign over my flat and all proceeds from the sale and pay them into his American bank account. A third nightmarish thought consisted of a putsch organised by all the men in my life (if they can laughingly be called that) in which I would be committed, first Mrs Rochester style, to the psychiatric unit of the Royal Free in Hampstead and would next be seen swathed in grey blankets, my dead face invisible to my persecutors as I was taken to be cremated and consigned to a soon-to-be forgotten history.

So a Note to Sugar Mummies: before you go looking for youth and love and happiness, ensure your assets are safe and protected from unscrupulous property dealers and ex-ex-Marxist husbands with overseas accounts and multinational lawyers. Any creditors should be paid off and dismissed; a company should be formed before advantage can be taken of the uncertain status of a Sugar Mummy purchasing gifts for her young lover. The uncertainty of his own duration with her is liable to cause problems when it comes to the return of such gifts in the event of a split.

Is that clear? Keep away from promises and legal arrangements made in the name of love, or you may end up without a roof over your head. Domicile abroad, if you can: a situation where, like me, you find yourself a sitting duck in the middle of a West London property boom, is never to be envied. Move quickly and quietly: repatriate your companion, if necessary to St Lucia or Jamaica (even if this is not his place of origin: the British government will be grateful to you).

At all costs, look after yourself.

It's now ten in the morning and I'm in the sitting-room, chastened and holding my umpteenth mug of tea. The builders have gone quiet upstairs, so I'm praying they were doing a quick job for Mr Nyan and won't return.

Molly, who has the good grace not to look pleased with herself after her night with Howie, is working as ever on the unpublishable sequel to *GWTW,* and she is smoking energetically as she does so. We've been through the other Henry James novels in which I appear to have been trapped, and after *Washington Square* with the depressed and independence-seeking heroine (she's like anyone would be if they took the advice I just gave earlier: she kept her lolly and her virginity but the human cost was appalling; is it worth it?) we came to *Portrait of a Lady.* 'Alain is Gilbert Osmond', Molly says. She sets her coffee down on the little inlaid marquetry table I found in the market at Bergerac forty years ago (ouch!) and an unremovable stain appears. The Osmonds wouldn't have put up with Molly for long—Madame Merle, that sinister 'older woman' with a secret, would have banished her from the palazzo in Florence, where poor Isabel Archer discovered the folly of her choice of Gilbert as a husband. As she'd married him, all her money was his. 'Yes', Molly goes on, 'like Osmond, Alain worships beauty…'

'I know', I say miserably. And I must add, to Sugar Mummies one more time: don't be fooled by men who flaunt their love of beauty and rob you of your money as well as any chance of happiness.

'What on earth are they doing upstairs?' Molly

says, as a series of loud crashes—falling plaster, walls caving in, resound just above our heads. And she gives me a look which reminds me I have a long way to go before I return to sanity. 'This is in your part of the house—it must be next to your room… on the landing.' And she rushes out into the hall.

So the real world pulled me back in the end, although it took two of Molly's super-strength painkillers and a gulp of rum from the bottle Gloria and Wayne left here before she discovered she was giving him something she hadn't got and he felt he didn't exist.

'I think they're taking out the staircase', Molly says as she pokes her head round the door from the hall.

A Broken Home,
A Broken Heart

∞ 26 ∞

'Mr Nyan is in breach of his lease. I shall send a letter demanding that any changes made to the property by Mr Nyan without your consent as shareholder in the company must be redressed immediately. You tell me the staircase in your maisonette has been removed and an alternative means of accessing the upper floors installed…'

'A ladder', I say miserably.

I'm talking to my lawyer the splendid Mrs Xerxes on my mobile in the hall while Michael (Polish, bristling moustache, i-pod and phone much in evidence) and his mate Andrew, also Polish, boiler-man (so I presume from the bunch of pipes that dangles from his hands and the unwelcome

169

sound of gushing water from upstairs) climb and descend the ladder with an agility which will certainly be seen to be lacking at my age.

'I'm not sure I can even get up to my room', I say wimpishly into my Nokia, while registering that the battery is failing: why does today have to be one of those days, when yesterday was another and the one before as well—black days standing like the witches in Macbeth and twiddling their thumbs on seeing me: 'This way evil comes!'

But what have I really done to deserve all this rotten luck? I've forgotten the First Rule for Sugar Mummies—don't blame yourself, a habit that comes from all the years of 'letting people down', i.e. late at school to pick up (Yes, I have a son, but he's in New Zealand, 'To get as far away as possible from home' as Molly likes to say, and I can't help agreeing with her); and the Second Rule—fight against the assumption you're being scatty. This a disease of old women, who are assumed by every man who meets them to have forgotten their own names, let alone the way to Roehampton or whatever—and generally being to blame for anything unpleasant that comes along.

'You must call the council at once', booms Mrs Xerxes from my failing phone.

So if all this is not my fault, whose is it? Surely it is I who have dithered and not told Crookstons since my discovery early in the morning that I had no intention of selling my flat, this omission leading to Mr Nyan's madly premature building works? It *must* be my fault that a fabulously valuable property in sought-after W9 is rapidly becoming unsaleable—for many months at least—in the hands of a gang of Polish workers while the lawsuit on which Mrs Xerxes will clearly insist drags on? We might as well rename ourselves Bleak House. I've been 'scatty' and let everyone down, most of all myself.

But I know what I'm trying to do, and it's not anything nice. I'm trying to pin the blame on someone else.

You must have guessed—it's Alain. Here is a list of his crimes: (1) being vague: hanging around without committing—to me, to a slice of equity in a future place to live; but not committing to me is worse; (2) muddying the waters even more by dragging his wife into the equation. Three into a shoebox won't go; (3) causing suspicion: is he in with Stefan Mocny; are they both about to skin me and, having done so, leave me skint?

Another unpleasant metaphor comes to mind:

that Stefan and Alain (yes, I accuse him: the Gestapo are after you now, Alain) and Mr Nyan are actually planning to launder money through me. I can hear the gurgle of long-neglected pipes on the floor above and it feels as if they're directly connected to my guts. *It's my money you're washing through me,* I want to shout. 'Turn off the tap. Let me live like I did before any of this happened…'

But you never can go back to the past. This is particularly illustrated by the sudden appearance of, of all people, Howie the Ex at the top of the ladder with only the bath-sheet knotted round him. Both Michael and Andrew, who are hanging bat-like through holes in the ceiling, stop sawing and banging and wait to see what's going to happen next.

'I was just going down to the kitchen', Howie says as he turns with surprising agility on the top rung of the ladder and descends painlessly (there's one less tragic accident to contemplate, at least). 'The canteen. The caddy', he continued in a pompous I-was-once-butler-to-Diana-Princess-of-Wales voice, 'it seemed to me that both had suffered serious losses since—well—since our wedding. The insurance is in place, I imagine?'

This is when I snapped. A voice sang in my ears. I felt myself turning bright red, all the symptoms of impending stroke and heart attack, so often pored over in the newspapers, threatened to despatch me (and some would say not before time) to the bizarrely positioned undertakers in Westbourne Grove (bizarre because the handbag and perfume shops now surrounding the long-established Kenyons seem positioned to tempt with reminders of worldly follies and extravagances, whereas before the new fashionability of Notting Hill and northwards, the odd bookmaker and fish-and-chip shop in Westbourne Grove served as indicators of the probability of a better life after death than in the years antecedent to it).

'I'm *off*', I yelled (a threat seldom very worrying from a Woman Past her Prime (unless she is the Sugar Mummy of the Recipient, of course): but neither Michael nor Andrew, chatting and laughing in Polish now that Howie has disappeared into the kitchen to count the teaspoons, have any knowledge of my financial affairs. Of course, Howie himself may have plans to remarry me—except he knows there isn't a chance.

So here I am. I'm *off*—i.e. on my front steps, having banged the front door really hard behind me. My mobile springs to life for an instant, and I can hear the tinny whisper of Mrs Xerxes. Then nothing. I'm leaving home forever. What am I going to do?

Alain is standing by his red car looking as if he's been there for hours. 'Are we going out looking for somewhere?' he says.

Glimmer of Hope

ை 27 ை

Now I'm really in a pickle. My home will shortly be uninhabitable—I've heard about these developers, cowboy space-thieves. In Notting Hill they buy two top flats in a building, box in the staircase down to the ground and sell a 'maisonette' to a City wanker for millions, having bagged the share of freehold space belonging to the other flats on the way down.

People don't sue, they haven't the time or money—and nor, I must confess, have I. (I can see the letter from the bank—there's no such thing as a bank manager nowadays as everyone knows, but my bank seems to have trained up a particularly ferocious virtual example, who throws in extra charges like he wants jam yesterday and jam the day before and more lashings of jam, all for an overdraft they know I'll pay off one day).

I'll start by sleeping on the sofa at home. (Think of the refugees trying to get to the Canaries, Molly will say as she does whenever I complain about discomfort, so Kurds/ Moldovians/ any of the miserable people suffering appalling conditions in flooded/ sun-baked camps will be brought forth if I moan about the second-hand Ikea settee Henrietta Shaw made me take out of one of the flats she was refurbishing—too Chav, she said. I can use the downstairs lavatory—why the hell didn't I put in a shower when I bought the flat?)

Then I won't be able to stay, due to builders encroaching on the remaining part of my flat.

'How are you today?' Alain asks me.

We're driving along at about fifteen miles an hour, just how I like it and I suppose the caution is due to the fact that even in the fairly early morning Alain may have had drinks or drugs (like many of my generation I know quite a bit about the former but have only a vague idea of a psychedelic whirl going round in the head of a younger person who uses drugs. So it's lucky we're going at the speed of a funeral cortège—the one with black horses and plumes, that is.

'I'm fine', I say.

How can I explain to Alain that he is a major suspect in the case of the bankrupting of a Sugar Mummy by prior arrangement with Mr Nyan, the man so busily expanding as we drive along? How can I even ask if Alain's friend and co-builder/decorator Stefan Mocny believes I'm about to buy the house in Hormead Road once the cash is 'freed up' by Crookstons on a sudden completion? I remember I signed a lengthy-looking contract at Crookstons that day after lunch at La Speranza—oh God, oh God, did I actually sign away my flat on that day—or at least grant the final decisions on the sale, along with a vast commission to Crookstons, so 'in all good faith', as they would put it, they sold to Mr Nyan, all above board and signature attached, by an idiot, a Sugar Mummy without a grey cell in her head? Me.

Am I the owner of a ludicrously expensive, deeply unattractive house without a view of the muggings and murders on the canal towpath but within striking distance (ha ha) of the gangs that go from house to house, knife in hand? Has the house even been surveyed? But if Crookstons can fake a signed name on a lease, as they notoriously can, then a bent surveyor is par for the course.

I hope, I pray, I hope a hundred times over, that Alain isn't involved in all of this. And I look back with a self-hatred that even I had never been capable of, on my fantasies of life in that awful house, a threesome with rent thrown in from the middle floor… Please! I've been living in cloud cuckooland.

'Actually, it looks rather nice', Alain is saying.

The House of Our Dreams

᷁ 28 ᷁

So here I am, on the corner of a street that is God-knows-where, but it has a nice country, villagey feel to it, with a large church and just a few houses, all of them a sort of greyish/ yellowish brick with pretty windows and window-boxes. We seem to have been driving for hours and I haven't noticed which direction we're going in, so it could be Stockwell or Brixton, one of those 'forgotten' streets where Henrietta Shaw likes to boast she's brought the Languedoc to south London, or some such rubbish.

I haven't been looking because quite frankly I'm so petrified by the Hormead/ home mess I'm in that all I've been able to do is stare at Alain's profile—not a punishing thing to do, I admit—and it certainly takes one's mind off the really pressing problems. But now he's slowed down and he's said he likes one of these houses, the one leaning right up against the church as if some long-ago vicar had wanted to settle there and decided to build right under the Victorian stained-glass window.

There's a board outside the house saying 'For Sale. Barringtons'.

I don't know why or how one's luck changes suddenly on a certain day. I read the horoscopes and like everyone else I forget them as soon as the eye has ranged over the clichéd prose—perhaps the habit of propping a celebrity next to a star sign is off-putting. The grinning figures of Tony Blair or Mick Jagger are quite enough to make one dismiss the idea of good or bad luck. These people knew where they were going from the start. Or maybe *not* believing in the stars is another form of superstition: if you haven't an inkling of what is said to be going to happen, then maybe something good will.

At least Alain is quite changed by the sight of this little, three-storey house. He almost jumps out of the car and I see he has energy but doesn't often care to use it (Ponce! Molly's voice whistles in my ear) and I see, too, that he is drawn first to the church, a lifetime of sightseeing in the Lubéron or the

Camargue the probable reason for this.

As Alain crawls round the great grey edifice of St Theodora (the name of the church is proclaimed in weather-worn letters on a wooden placard above the boarded-up door) he goes so far as to try the rusty iron handle of the main portal (he certainly doesn't know London, he lives in the rural past in France) and I, standing at the foot of the flight of stone steps leading in front of the house Barringtons wants to sell, begin to feel as if something different and momentous is taking place.

It's hard to describe happiness, when half the world denies its existence and the other half, without producing any evidence, insists that the pursuit of this desirable (non-existent, like love in the language of Lacan?) quality is the most important aim in life. But it's also true that unhappiness becomes easier to define when the possible other thing comes along. And the strange part is that it's a house—a simple, not-very-exciting house—that is most likely to trigger this change, if people's testimony is to be believed. 'We know this is a happy house', 'I fell in love with the house as soon as I saw it and have been happy here ever since'— again, these appear at first to be clichés and are certainly sales talk—but they're sincere too.

And the atmosphere—the environmental climate—whatever you like to call it, made me feel I could be happy here, and that Alain would be happy here as well. (Idiot! Molly whistles right into my ear.)

A hedge of wild lavender in the stubby front garden, the back garden at the side of the house (the church really is bang up against the house) and in the side/back garden a shed, half-rotting but roofed and looked down on by the blues and reds and purples of St Theodora's stained-glass robes.

'A kiln', Alain says. And as he speaks the sun comes out and the day grows hotter, while a traffic warden, staring idly at us while we stand back and admire the house/church from beside the little red car, wanders down the street to give us a ticket.

'We won't be a minute', I say to the warden and, believe it or not, he smiles at me and saunters on.

What's happening here? Will I have three wishes, like in the fairytale (I remind myself not to become The Old Woman in the Vinegar Bottle, who wished for larger and larger houses until her demand for a papal palace sent her back to the vinegar bottle for eternity). Will I be like poor Gloria, who wished for fidelity from her Object of Desire—and got it for all of six months, but then asked for the impossible, that he get a job and support them both as proof of his love for her? Does a 'run of luck' exist, the streak every gambler prays for? I've been offered, after all, a vast sum on my flat... Alain is here and we've found a house. Three is enough, surely.

That's when I realised that I'd never been happy in my flat. This is the place for me.

Warning to Sugar Mummies

This is the crunch time for Sugar Mummies who are about to commit their all to a shared venture which may prove unsuccessful.

Questions that need urgently to be asked:

If you move to this new house with your Object of Desire, will you know anyone/ have friends in the area? Sugar Mummies left to contemplate the isolation and panic which can set in if stranded in an unfamiliar part of the city must take the possibility of this occurring into account. You will no longer be recognised at the chemist; you will be a stranger in the local shops; you will be surrounded by people who have no interest

in you. At an advanced age, this is not
agreeable.

Can you really afford the house? Suppose
there are huge repair bills, can you pay?
Will there be employment for both of you if
you move?

I present the above questions simply in order to
avoid the anger and resentment of ex-Sugar
Mummies all determined to sue in the event that
their house move with a Loved One has not gone
well. I cannot be held responsible for the ill-
considered actions of others.

But as for us. Well, as you have probably guessed,
there were no two ways about it.

Alain stood staring at the façade of the little,
grey/yellow house as if bewitched. He also stared at
the kiln, and with his eyes he retraced the path from
the kiln down to the back (or side) basement door,
which leads into a low-ceilinged but independently
situated room from which he could (I saw this with
less pleasure) slip in and out whenever he felt the
need. We didn't have to say anything.

The traffic warden, looking slightly less friendly
than the first time (the second wish in a fairytale

often won't work as well as the first) walked up towards us and we got into the car and drove off as slowly as subaqueous creatures so deep on the ocean bed that we were no longer able to see.

My mobile jumped into life (perhaps we were on a hill—but where?) and I rang Barringtons.

'No, I'm afraid not, Madam.' The man had a cross, don't-bother-me voice and I felt the first stirrings of remorse at my longing for the house.

'Why not?' I heard myself sound just like the rich women who used to come into my little shop off the North End Road. Was this 'final' decision to accept the offer on my flat and buy the magic house turning me into an angry Sloane?

'The vendors are away until next Wednesday', the voice came back to me. 'In Ireland', its owner added unnecessarily.

'And I'll have gone back to Bandol by then', Alain said as we drove at a snail's pace round the corner and stopped.

And we were here. You may have guessed. We'd only been round the corner all along. I wouldn't be lonely anyway if I moved! And just as I was thinking that Alain must have got lost on the way there and had driven round in circles, Howie appeared on the doorstep.

'Yo', he cried to Alain, and he looked hard at me. 'Coming in for a drink?'

I'll Pay, I'll Pay

❧ 29 ❧

Well, the good luck went on. I'll be getting a windfall from my bank or building society next, thanking me for being such a special customer 'and here's £500'. Only joking.

We didn't accept Howie's kind invitation to come into my flat and drink my drink. We went, as if we knew that good luck turns bad if you don't fertilise it, give it at least a modicum of TLC, to Crookstons at the bottom of the road. The man there, distinctly provincial, Yorkshire accent and all, compared to the Notting Hill variety, looked up something on the screen and said the sale was proceeding smoothly. I asked when I'd be paid (I fancied a faint tremor from Alain when I asked the all-important

question, the one whose answer will house him—
and no mention of the lovely Claire so far, I'm
thankful to note—and will provide this elusive
'happiness' for the rest of our lives—well his,
anyway. I will have died from old age, if nothing
worse).

Then I remembered my solicitor. But it appeared
that Crookstons has thought of everything. Mrs
Xerxes' name is on their files, due to a complaint I
made at the time that Mr Nyan bought the upstairs
maisonette—she dealt with the matter—a minor
one but unpleasant, as it consisted of Mr Nyan's
washbasin emptying on to the floor above my bed,
and water crashing through the ceiling on to my
new duvet. My then-TV was also inundated along
with the video library, and thankfully, as I recall,
Gone With The Wind was unplayable until finally
replaced by Molly.

'Completion in three weeks', said the rosy-
cheeked estate agent.

That's all right then, I think. I won't be expected
to 'free up' funds for the purchase of the house in
Hormead Road, one of my greatest dreads being
that I would find myself in possession of the horrible
house, along with Stefan Mocny's cock, which
haunts me and always will, a part of the interior

decoration of that disastrous building.

'No, we're going to buy the lovely, yellow/grey house.' 'Barringtons?' says the Crookstons man incredulously. 'That house has been on the market for over a year.'

'Why is that?' I almost feel proud of him: that was Alain speaking. He can if he wants to, you see.

'The asking price is unrealistic', snaps the once jolly countryman-turned-Fagin type, eyes burning with avarice and hate, hands playing nervously on his desk.

'How much is it?' I ask.

Oh, surely I could have avoided this one. If my poxy maisonette is 'worth' seven hundred grand plus and it's on two floors—or was until Mr Nyan made his early days move and turned it into a one-floor bedsit—then the three-storeyed house around the corner must be worth more. (How could I not have recognised the church? Huge and grey, it's the elephant in the neighbourhood and Alain must think me a complete philistine for not knowing St Theodora's when I walked bang into it.)

The reply when it comes is almost a relief. 'Eight hundred thousand, nine hundred and ninety-five pounds', intones Crookston man. 'There is an offer,

I believe, on the property, which has structural problems.'

'I'll offer the asking price', I bellow, aware that Alain is looking at me with the surprise and admiration reserved for an heiress who keeps the extent of her funds secret until it is expedient to reveal them.

'You wish us to negotiate the purchase for you?' says Yorkshireman, now miraculously restored from conman and viper. 'We are happy to do so.'

'Yes', I say. I come over pompous—we *must* have that house. There are no two ways about it. I'll die if we don't get it…

'I shall inform my solicitor immediately', I say.

Don't ask. I've no idea where the extra hundred thousand will come from after the sale of my flat, to pay for dream house. Maybe the bank will lend it to me, ha ha. But I still consider my luck to be 'in'—even if the owners of dream house are really the ones having a lucky day. They might as well stay in Ireland and dance with the leprechauns after finding a Crazy Jane such as myself who is willing to hand them a crock of gold.

Holding my head high, and after assurances to Crookstons that I will be in touch shortly, we continue on one of the lengthy but tiny distance drives which takes us back home.

And I'm right; good fortune smiles on us when we're there too. For one thing, the house is empty and I mean the whole house. The builders have gone, leaving a half-boxed-in new staircase leading upwards, and, through one of the holes in the ground-floor ceiling, a spiral staircase in imitation 'old' cast-iron (in fact, plastic). This is clearly meant to service the lower maisonette and I can use it to 'access' my room.

But I don't want to. With a new confidence I stride ahead of Alain to the kitchen—which has no one there, too: no Howie, no Molly, no Gloria back from St Lucia with her tales of woe amongst the Pitons. There is wine, both red and white, and we start in on it. Ham and salami in the fridge. Yesterday's bread.

We're going to end up being very happy indeed, Alain and me.

Gone

☞ 30 ☜

It's strange how love puts a kind of squeezer on the stomach so even the smallest mouthful feels like climbing (and then being forced to eat) Mount Everest. There's very little ham—Howie has clearly been at it: telltale signs are fatty, bread-crumbed edges all gone, a habit which accounts for a tubby appearance at the best of times; and salami, just a handful of slices left, rinds carefully tucked under the greaseproof-paper wrapping. A tired-looking casserole (definitely not exchanged for sexual favours, as I read is the custom amongst the literati) sits on the gas hob. Neither Alain nor I have warmed it up, for fear it's Molly's rabbit Provençale (a short description was enough to deter him, though he's clearly hungry and I'm not).

There's even a candle, stored since the last power cut, in the drawer where a messy assortment of Elastoplast guards against bleeding in event of a minor injury (OK, the increasingly frequent stumble or fall, accompaniment of old age and on no account to be admitted) and paracetamol, which I see Alain look at in an interested way when I slide open the drawer to extract the kitchen scissors. The candles are irritatingly stuck together, perhaps the victims of a lesbian orgy in Molly's younger, Sapphic days.)

And—God, how embarrassing—there's a copy of my will. I wondered where I'd put it, last time I had a clear-out in my room, and I suppose I'm relieved to see it (I'm not, actually), but it does remind me at least that I need to make a new one. Or should I slide it under the used silver foil (really, who wants remnants of last Christmas's turkey?) and sales-bargain packets of clingfilm that must belong to Molly's Hausfrau phase shortly after the Greek passions went out of the door.

Here I am, holding the will because paralysed with indecision (what's new?), and I think not for the first time what a wonderful, calming presence Alain has. With me being a hysteric and him practically catatonic, we couldn't be better matched.

I'm especially grateful that he makes no reference to the obvious identity of the document I'm holding as if I'm about to go down in the *Titanic* with my will clutched to my bosom. That's the thing with Alain: he's either super-tactful or he just doesn't care. It doesn't really matter which. But it would be a dereliction of my duty in writing this cautionary tale for Sugar Mummies if I neglected to extrapolate on so important a matter as a Last Will and Testament—indeed, a life or death matter for the Sugar Mummy, who must conceal or reveal her intentions only after extremely careful deliberation:

Never allow the Object of Desire to bring up the subject of inheritance/ his chances of having somewhere to live etc. after you die/bank loans and mortgage arrangements which require (a) marriage; (b) surrender of title deed to your property; (c) added clauses in incomprehensible jargon; (d) the inclusion of relatives (who turn out to be past lovers) in your list of bequests. A Venetian mirror left to Marilyn can transpire to consist of a secret code involving your estate, and rob you of all your assets in your lifetime.

If the existence of a will is leaked or the document inadvertently discovered by your man, destroy it in front of him and immediately write another in which everything goes to him, his name appearing in large letters at every possible opening in the will. Leave this around the house (suggestion: on hall table, unmissable as it will lie there with the mail; in your boudoir, i.e. on your dressing-table, engagingly smeared with mascara and eye shadow; or (yes, he'll only find it if he helps around the house, but its positioning may urge him to do housework at last, depending, of course, on how long he thinks you have to live) in the kitchen drawer. Ensure your actual will is safely with your solicitor.

This leads to the most crucial point when discussing the Last Statement of Your Intentions towards your Object of Desire. *Do not leave* anything sharp or dangerous lying around, for obvious reasons. Lifers are released after only a brief period of incarceration these days, and taking that route may well be considered worthwhile by him, depending, of course, on the extent of your wealth.

♋ ♋ ♋ ♋

So it's a candle-lit dinner in the kitchen of what I will look back on one day with nostalgia (maybe, what for?) or possibly amnesia, as it occurs to me that I've been here eight years but can't remember anything of significance about the period. (Maybe, when you grow old, there's nothing memorable about *you*, so that same blurring of fact and fantasy occurs when you try to look back at the past.

But I don't feel nostalgic tonight. Alain has succeeded in making very strong coffee—God knows how, when the Nescafe I give Molly (mean, I know; I keep freshly roasted beans for myself alone, when I can afford them) and a bag of something with a chicory smell (Howie) seem to be all there is. But Alain's French, so he probably unearthed the Real Thing in some untouched cupboard—along with a half bottle of cooking brandy, which tastes surprisingly good. I've slipped the will back into the drawer, under a porn mag (must be Howie: how *dare* he?) and I have to say that I wondered a bit at the way the paracetamols had all gone, with the exception of half a panel. I didn't take them, unless I've really become scatty, so it must have been Alain: do they plus brandy plus two bottles of supermarket wine account for the smile (that smile again) which he's beaming across the table at me?

I don't care. Tonight, even if it means the plastic spiral, we're going up to my room. Even if Molly has set up *Gone…* I'll simply smash the plasma screen and live happily ever after with Alain…

Well, you were expecting it, weren't you? No, the doorbell didn't ring—not then, anyway. Nor did the phone, which sat on the kitchen table looking as if it had a spell on it, a strict instruction from 'on high' not to ring.

It was Alain. He was still sitting smiling and gazing (it was thrilling at the time) straight into my eyes, when he suddenly leapt to his feet and started pulling something out of his pocket, and then he went off like an alarm clock, if you can imagine such a cool person leaping in the air and emitting bell-like peals—and then I saw that what he'd pulled from his pocket was an air ticket.

And then I remembered, he'd said perfectly clearly in the little red car as we drove back that he had to go back to Bandol. Of course, he hadn't said when; how could I have dreamt it would be tonight?

But it is. Alain has gone. And the only words he said as I ran desperately up into the ruined hall after him were 'I'll be back'.

But will he? And when?

Stefan's Back

♋ 31 ♋

'No peace for the wicked!' May's favourite saying and now I see why she'd mutter it whenever I'd done what most children/ adolescents do, i.e. run away (OK only as far as the local shop selling ice-creams and then run back again) and, more serious, run away to Soho aged fourteen (arrested half-way there and driven back) while my parents were away and May had to answer for the consequences.

It's being bad from the very start of your life that makes you extra depressed at a time like this. God questions me as I lie in bed and wish (a first, this) that Howie and Molly were in the spare room and there was some human life on the planet. As the Civil War shows Scarlett in deep widow's weeds and

Ashley walks about exhausted (rather like Alain, I can't help thinking, but that makes me cry again) I try to answer the Almighty's interrogations (this section to be skipped by Sugar Mummies, out of pure boredom if nothing else).

God: You knew Alain was married. You had even accepted hospitality from his wife. Did you not foresee the trouble that would arise if you insisted on trying to make him end his marriage?

Answer: How can I tell God that I'd been perfectly happy to accept a threesome? It doesn't sound polite somehow, even if God himself is sharing a sort of Hormead Road (three levels: Heaven, Limbo and Hell) with the other two members of the Holy Trinity? (At least, if I'd gone for that dreadful set-up, I'd have been getting rent from Limbo. But, on the ground floor, I'd have been in Hell.)

God: It is a venal sin to offer bribes in return for sexual favours. You must do penance for this.

Answer: What sexual favours? Bitter laugh. Maybe God really doesn't know the difference between celibacy and clitoral orgasm. But why should he? He impregnated the Virgin Mary, after all, by sending a messenger who informed the mother-to-be that this was her new ranking.

Confessions of a Sugar Mummy

So no more disapproval for Sugar Mummies who don't want to find God when they've just discovered sex with their Object of Desire. But an instruction or two doesn't come amiss at the other kind of time—when the Object has returned to connubial bliss and you have no idea when, if ever, he will come back to you:

> Don't call him, however great the temptation. Sod's Law—and God's too for all I know—is that his wife will answer the phone and you will be caught, a bunny boiler whose paws are caught in a trap.

> Do add up where your finances are at. Have you made any foolish offers recently, for things you really can't afford? Cancel them now.

I might as well own up that adhering to these two rules was impossible for me. I thought first about the dream house—I was honest with myself—a voice even said loudly somewhere above my head that of course I knew perfectly well that I couldn't afford it. I was about to be paid a fortune for my flat and I still wouldn't be able to afford it.

But I have to be there with Alain. He can sell something, surely… But then I see a handful of tiles at £3.50 each (or even a true Tuscan tile at £10) and I know we're just not going to be able to raise the money. I might as well stay here, then.

This is where all my dreams end and the lovely house just has to go up in smoke with them.

Why should I bother to go on living?

♋ ♋ ♋ ♋

The bad thing about hope is not that it springs eternal (it's hype that does that) but that it's so hard to give it up. Every sound or remark—or, in the case of horoscopes, strange weather patterns and all the other encouragers of false hope, raisers of expectations and dashers of overflowing cups—betoken a coming joy. You are thrilled at the connections and correspondences between things; you're a magician, a pal of John Dee in Elizabethan England; you're a Neo-Platonist; you belong to the School of Night.

I'm just thinking all this—at the same time, it must be said, as discovering a wart tucked in neatly by my right eye and, hell's bells, another down on the fourth finger of my left hand (any symbolism here?—it's the wedding ring finger, natch)—I'm just brooding on the alliance of hope and magic when the noise goes off downstairs. It's like a parakeet choking on a cough lozenge, shrill and mellifluous at the same time. What the hell can it be?

If those distinctly unhoped-for signals of old age, the warts, have made me a witch (I refuse to check yet for a grey beard) they certainly seem to have rendered me braver, less—OK—full of bathos than I was an hour or so ago just after Alain sprang into the air and ran like the last ray of hope right out of my life.

If it's a burglar down there making some kind of multicultural cry of triumph at finding the silver laid out by Howie on the step of the stair by the downstairs loo—now why did Howie have to do that? Why was I so overcome with grief at Alain's departure that I left the forks and spoons etc. ready for the next taker?—then I'm going down to greet that burglar. I'll give him a piece of my mind. And it occurs to me, as I shrug on an old tweed jacket and shout 'Who's there?' down the plastic spiral into the hall, that my voice is lower and gruffer than usual. Is this why old women are feared and hated so much? Because under the witch disguise they've actually become men and so are rivals for power?

I didn't need to get as far as the front door, though. I hear a muffled electronic growl and then an ear-splitting click and the door swings open. I must have pressed a button, but what button; how dare Mr Nyan install this horrible entryphone without even consulting me? I could—and have— let just anybody in.

Hope gives a painful flicker somewhere inside my rib cage like acute indigestion. He's come back, he couldn't bear the thought of leaving me here even for one night—that kind of tosh. However, nothing would stop the voice and accompanying pang: It's Alain! He doesn't want to go back and pack up; he wants to start a new life with me. And, despite myself, as old novels used to say, I receive a clear picture of Dream House, border of wild lavender by the off-its-hinges front gate, side garden with shed, and all.

Now I'm at the top of the plastic spiral and I see the man standing at its foot like a knight in a cheaply illustrated fairy story is—well it wasn't Alain, for anyone who's chosen this book as a romantic turn-on, forget it—it was Alain's colleague Stefan Mocny. And here I am in my nightie, my new deep voice going higher and higher as I ask him what he wants and is Alain OK? (Another sign of thwarted hope: thinking the Object of Desire has been run over or was in a head-on crash when in fact he's got safely to the airport hours ago and is now relaxing in the plane with an in-flight magazine.)

Stefan Mocny seems surprised by my query, so ignores it. 'This spiral staircase is unsafe. Highly dangerous', he proclaims as he swings on and then off like an ape. 'Who put this in?' But then he grows thoughtful when I say Mr Nyan, and concedes that it may be 'just OK'. Well, thanks very much. Is it safe to use or not, I'm thinking, and how about poor Molly with her arthritis? Suppose it topples over when she tries to come down…

I didn't want to go back in the kitchen, which holds my last memories of Alain, and particularly the way he'd smiled and pulled the roll of clingfilm out of the drawer and wrapped it swiftly and efficiently (yes, those are the words) over the plate with the remains of the ham. 'I *can* do these things', he'd said, as I took the plate from him and put it in the fridge; and I knew he meant we were going to be together, no nonsense about a compromise. I found it rather sweet (toe-curling, Molly whistles in my ear).

Now Stefan Mocny is sitting where Alain sat. He's not getting the real coffee Alain made, he's lucky to get a Nescafe. 'I hope I haven't disturbed you', he says.

Hope on, I say to myself as the last remnants of my own hope—for love, for happiness, for all those things that might exist but probably do not, fly out through the iron grill gate on the window, into the night.

'Wanna tell ya', Stefan says, 'Claire—you know her, right?' And, as I nod wearily, 'She called tonight. I said there was no flat in sight yet, but I knew you'd commit to 29 Hormead Road, right?'

Cockmail

♋ 32 ♋

It's taken me two whole days to feel OK enough to go on describing that terrible night—the night Alain left and Stefan Mocny came round, and the world looked set to end pretty sharply (or I wanted it to end, the whole ruddy ball simply coming to a halt with its load of frauds and crooks and murderers and blackmailers).

Yes, Stefan Mocny can be described as a typical denizen of the world we live in today (I sound like my mother) and if you throw in rapist and torturer you're just upping his status, something he wouldn't mind at all, as 'these days' (my mother again) the more wicked you are, the more you're admired, even photographed and labelled a celebrity. Grind the faces of the poor? Now there's an old-fashioned concept, the poor don't even *have* faces any more, they're talked of at charity balls or by the chancellor in gold-plated rooms, but they don't exist one by one: they're not *people* any more. Steal and lie? You're a star. And so the list goes on, with hand-wringing and spin making the city like a gigantic washing-machine with all the dirty laundry going round to huge applause.

Mocny, the Bill Sykes of our new Victorian age, came round the side of the kitchen table and started fumbling with his flies (if that's what they're known as if it's a zip). There was an unpleasant bunch of black pubic hair sticking out under the fastener. How could he be a friend of Alain? flashes across my mind as he lumbers towards me, penis upright, a hot dog between the greasy bun of his thighs: why did they ever get on well together, or was it just a case of Me Artisan, You Mocny? Well, when he got to me I was paralysed, I just couldn't move. It's not an excuse, though the new rape judges would say I provoked it and he...

Oh God I can't write this. Suppose someone discovers it's me writing this book—imagine if Alain and Claire are doing a Google on a house in the south of France they might be able to afford to rent, and they come across my description of their work colleague… And worst of all, if they read about me: my pathetic efforts to pay an innocent husband (have these words ever been linked before?) to live with me, a superannuated Biba girl, in a flat so horrible that when you go there all thoughts of adultery vanish like summer snow.

Because I will have to buy 29 Hormead Road. It's true, and it's my machinations that have led to this. Walk on, Molly: I could kill her for looking smug a few days back. 'Sometimes it's better to be paying rent', as I agonised over the ludicrous price of Dream House and the apparent 'bargain' my flat has now become. I'm the old woman in a vinegar bottle indeed, a Sugar Mummy with all the sweetness gone, in a sea of greed and bitterness.

But I'm going to have to buy 29 Hormead Road because Stefan Mocny just blackmailed me into it. You'll just have to imagine my cry of disgust, sitting at the table with his Frankfurter cock just inches away from my mouth and its proprietor (I guess every part of Mocny is valued, surveyed and gains in value by the day) staring impassively down at me. 'Go on', his voice comes from miles away. 'Get a move on, I've a refurb in All Soul's Avenue that needs me, the roof collapsed.'

Oh God, where are you? I'm sorry, so sorry… and yet, seeing the jar of Colman's mustard on the kitchen table (Alain had refused it: he must go for those Moutarde de Meaux numbers with little peppercorns and mustard seeds all stuck together in a posh jar) I can't help bursting into hysterical laughter… Maybe it's to keep my mouth busy so I don't have to have oral sex with a repulsive developer… 'OK then.' Stefan pulls away, treating me to the unedifying sight of a shrinking sausage as it retreats into his jeans. 'I think I'll give Claire— that's Alain's wife as you know—a ring back. She'll want to know how we're progressing with 29 Hormead Road, won't she? But what she won't know is how you and Alain plan to live there— Claire won't like being a gooseberry, no way.'

Oh God again. So Stefan Mocny knows. But on second thoughts—and there wasn't much time for those just then—what does he know? After all, we're innocent, Alain and I… shamingly, Stefan must simply have seen me slobbering, ogling, whenever his old colleague, the 'tile man', was near.

Shaming and degrading. It couldn't be worse. But I can't allow Stefan to make that call. I can't lose Alain. I can't and won't.

It's a Stitch-Up

౦౦ 33 ౦౦

If I thought I had dark nights of the soul before, they were buttercup-yellow afternoons compared to what I'm going through now.

Alain has gone, I'm blackmailed by Stefan Mocny into buying you-know-where, that shit-hole down by the canal, and for all of the rest of my life I shall have to live there. ('You'll get a nice rent for the two empty flats', Molly says brightly. 'After all you've gone through you'll wish you were a tenant like me—a protected tenant.' And she gives the smug little harrumph that makes me want to kill her almost as much as I want to kill Stefan Mocny.

But what Molly says is true. Alain and Claire won't live at 29 Hormead Road—it just won't happen. I'll be there on my own, 'celebrating old age' as Virginia Ironside unconvincingly puts it (though she does advise covering the upper arms at all times).

I will be empty, like the other two flats let to interchangeable tenants—so empty in heart and soul. No one will call me, my inbox will be empty as all the people of my age I might count as friends are totally incapable of sending a text message. I will have nothing but my pension—wait a minute…

Stefan Mocny, before leaving with his newly zipped-up member for Willesden (no pun intended), hands me a legal-looking letter (from Crookstons, natch) with a description of 29 Hormead Road (perfect family house, etc.) and a price that seems familiar because—and even I, Granny Bovary with my head full of fantasies, recognise it after a while—because it *is* familiar: it's exactly the sum offered by Mr Nyan, the asking price for my maisonette here.

What the heck is going on?

Here's a brief word of advice to Sugar Mummies with failing memories:

If in a shop and unable to recall the sum mentioned by the salesgirl for your purchase,

rush to the other side of the department, fish
an extravagantly priced dress from the rail,
run back with it while holding the price tag
up to your eyes (see reference to Sugar
Mummies with age-related macular degeneration) and ask how much the two items
together will cost. Then subtract or add as
necessary and the memory of the price of the
original item will become clear.

With a house or flat, this is obviously impossible.
But a memory—false or true I cannot tell—does
come to me of Alain saying after we had left
Hormead Road (the time he pretended his hand was
a mobile phone; I thought that was terribly funny.
Oh stop it, Molly's brisk tones come to me) that
Stefan had told him the place was going cheap
because the owner was in deep financial trouble;
how cheap I certainly don't remember asking him.

So Stefan has bumped up the price! Stefan,
together with Crookstons, of course (they will make
it worth his while) will indeed wash Nyan's money
right through me. I'll be left exactly as I was before,
with nothing except a roof over my head—in this
case a roof I detest. ('You'll get the rent, Molly insists.
Where you are now is too weirdly laid out to let.')

And there's nothing I can do about it. Alain, I'm doing this for you! I am doing it to show the extent of my loyalty and affection…

'Oh, stop it', Molly says. This time it really is Molly and she's walked into my squalid bedroom— what's the point of making the bed if you're the only one for ever and ever who will sleep in it? And she's listening to my outpourings of grief with her usual sardonic expression. 'You're wanted on the phone', Molly says. (Molly hates mobiles and won't have one.) 'It's Henrietta Shaw. She says you left the last job unfinished and she's not going to settle up until you do it. The flat in Lots Road.'

'But they're going to demolish it', I groan. Everywhere is either horrible or ruined, each house or flat I've ever done up or lived in is a major disaster. 'You know', I say to Molly, 'in the year of the French Revolution the king—Louis XVI—just had one word written on each day in his diary…'

'What was that?' Molly snaps. 'Not a completion date for his appointment with the guillotine, I suppose?'

'No', I say. 'It was "rien".'

'It meant he had no sex the night before', Molly says. (She considers herself an expert on the French Revolution as well as *Gone With The Wind*.) 'I think that's rather funny, don't you?'

'I don't know', I say miserably.

'Well, that woman is still on the phone. She said she was short-staffed and she's got a job for you.'

'Not in her shop?' I say. The moan comes free with this one.

'Yes. What's wrong with that, even if they pay OAP rates?' Molly comes back at her sharpest. 'It's *work,* Scarlett, it'll do you good.'

And as she leaves the room, she flicks the DVD remote. Vivien Leigh and Clark Gable are on a paddleboat going up the Mississippi. She swoons in his arms and the ghastly theme music swells…

It's the first time I've been grateful for the Polish builders when they get the drill going and position it directly overhead.

Midsummer Night's Sexpectations Revisited

≈ 34 ≈

October. Bits of summer are still sticking around—it's hot and muggy sometimes but getting cooler at night. You no longer feel as if you've been flown to Mauritius and dumped on an island with a rising sea level, a submerged airstrip (you're the last flight in) and only old novels by Jilly Cooper (funny, but you've read them) and Rachel Cusk (life can't be as bad as this, but it is) in the abandoned beach house.

No, a semblance of sanity has returned with the nocturnal chill and falling leaves, and like migrating birds those who can't bear unfairness—those who liked you but didn't know what to do about your terrible predicament (sex and property in West

London)—arrive in their flocks to advise and assist you. After all, we belong in a temperate climate: surely, as my valiant geese and swans say, as they honk overhead, there must be a way to get out of the pickle you're in. And there was. Mrs Xerxes took over the flat I had so intemperately sold (but that was in the hot summer, the global swing away from rationality and into madness) and, as Molly describes her, like a kindly bird in an Aristophanes comedy she dealt with Mr Nyan. The council was informed of his building works, all done without planning permission and he suffered the humiliation and expense of taking out the plastic spiral and replacing the original staircase.

Then, I believe also engineered by Mrs Xerxes, a new company was formed, in which I had the majority of shares, as well as being appointed landlord of the building. All transactions must be above board and approved or vetoed by the company. This got rid of Mr Nyan, who had no wish to be registered as a shareholder, identifiable to the tax office. He moved out in August, young Bill carrying his Buddhas and metal trunks down the reconstructed stairs. Molly and I went down to the new bar 'W9' in the suddenly fashionable Shannon Road to celebrate.

You may ask who the Hell is Bill? This is how I saw him again I've unkindly referred to him as resembling a Nazi concentration camp guard earlier, and I unreservedly apologise to him. He's an angel, and how he worked all those years for Stefan Mocny I do not know (yes, he's that one). This is what happened.

I'm in the sitting-room just after starting work in Lots Road. I'm exhausted after a day at Henrietta Shaw's shop (not least tiring are her meaningful questions about Alain: 'What was going on?' 'You're a sly one', etc., which drove me almost berserk with irritation). If you're trying to forget someone, you don't want their name where you had once hoped their tongue would be, i.e. rammed down your throat. And here, as I'm prone on the sitting-room sofa with a cup of tea kindly brought by Molly, are a few words to Sugar Mummies who are desperately trying to get rid of the memory after an unfortunate encounter with an Object of Desire:

> Do not discuss the relationship and how you
> know it has ended or whether he wants/ does
> not want/ to end it. Doing so will produce
> pangs of regret, and these can be the worst
> pangs of all.

On the same level, do not write/ ring/ text/
fax/ email your decision to shake the sugar
from your shoes for once and for all and
head for retirement in Torquay/ Tangier/ ex-
council flat in Clacton. As you speak you will
probably cry—only to discover his new
Mummy/wife/fiancée/hooker answered the
phone anyway and is lying on a comfortable
bed in the flat she has worked so hard to
furnish, watching *To Die For* for the
hundredth time (you can hear *Season of the
Witch* as it builds in the background.)

On no account give a payoff/ goodbye
present/ photos of you both together to the
departing Object of Desire. It is hurtful if
they return for more, and devastating if a
photo album is found in a local car boot sale.

So here I am. I'm in my flat and I'm not going to sell
it, a huge improvement on when Alain was here and
midsummer grabbed us both and wouldn't let us go.
I now know that even if I'm offered the same price
or more for it, it's fairy gold. I mean, where am I
going to go? (OK, I'm one of the lucky ones, you

may say: I don't *have* to sell, to get rid of debts, to pay off a mortgage for once and for all.) But after the Hormead Road and Maygrove Road experience, I really can't see where I could live—and anyway what's wrong with where I am?

Bill bangs the knocker (I got rid of Mr Nyan's throttled-budgie door chime as soon as he'd gone) and Molly gives him a beer and he starts in. I wish Bill was my type, but he's not: so Aryan, so unmoving and straightforward—none of Alain's tortured silences for him—but then I don't want to talk about Alain ever again. After trying to call him on the night Stefan Mocny came round and wiggled his thing at me, Claire answered, natch, and I burst into tears, and Alain came to the phone, but all he said was 'Oh Scarlett' and so I hung up—after all that I will never again say or hear the name Alain. That I promise and it's for keeps.

Bill said he wanted to tell me something before it was too late. So Molly sat forward and I pulled my aching legs off the sofa (are we oldies really meant to retire in our seventies when we paid our National Insurance stamps all those years in order to be looked after when we turn sixty?) and Bill was saying that 29 Hormead Road wouldn't be a good buy for me—and he didn't know where to look when he said this, because obviously if I ratted on him he'd lose his £100 a day job with Stefan Mocny.

I couldn't tell Bill that his boss had blackmailed me into saying I'd buy the house from hell so I said nothing and there was a long silence.

'Twenty-nine Hormead Road belongs to Stefan', Bill said at last.

ʒ ʒ ʒ ʒ

So there you are. Stefan and Crookstons were planning on a massive profit out of me when the sale of my flat to Mr Nyan went through. I had been saved by the skin of my teeth.

'Alain said you liked that house by the church', Bill went on; and I felt myself go red in the face. I want to recover, I felt like screaming at him—that name cannot be mentioned in this house! (For I knew the path to survival led to simply not caring what Stefan told Claire, what Alain thinks of any of it, what Claire believes.) 'They're a pack of cards!' I heard myself saying aloud while Molly giggled.

'I know the house, scouting for Stefan', Bill says, and he too blushes—must be a symptom of Boom Disease.

'And?' I say. I have to know, I thought of Dream House so often…

'It's in need of demolition and total rebuilding', Bill says. 'Been on the market about two years. The owners have emigrated to Ireland and they're thinking of selling just the site.'

'I see', I say.

He'll Be Back

∽ 35 ∽

It's nearly Hallowe'en and I'm writing this in Henrietta's shop—thankfully she's not here, probably headed up to trendy W9 to see some clients, and I hear the rockets go off early as if to tell us that this is indeed the season of the witch: black nights that come down suddenly in the middle of the afternoon, storm-level rain and hurricane-force winds, every London garden a blasted heath.

I am not a witch; Molly rubbed some witch hazel on my warts and they slunk off. I am not a witch; since Alain left I've had no sense of magic spells (I think they came from Stefan Mocny. Anyone would have felt a pricking of their thumbs when seeing *him* zoom down the road on his Harley Davidson).

I've witnessed the look on the faces of poor people in an about-to-be requisitioned house when Stefan walked in, bodyguarded by two men from Crookstons, holding aloft the contract only the weak and foolish will sign. Stefan, who engineered a fake future for Alain and me in a sham house…

So if I'm not a witch, what am I? The question remains as imponderable as before. Can I be visible when I choose? I hope so, I've booked a makeover at the new beauty spa at the end of Saltram Crescent, and Molly is planning a party—in my flat, as her one-room rental won't fit in all the people from her publishing firm that she wants to invite. ('You'll find someone else, I'm going to ask Greg to the party', Molly says. I wish she wouldn't.)

What does it mean, ageing gracefully? And is ageing disgracefully just a matter of wearing purple? If so, how sad.

Or maybe we can just be people. Give up our seat in the bus to young pregnant women, mend cars, cook great meals when we feel like it…

I wander round Henrietta's poky little shop, with its kilims and ancient Cypriot earthenware and wall-paint samples in dowdy Heritage greys and greens. And as I do I hear the letterbox in the hall bang up and down: junk mail, letters and bills for the impractical Henrietta... and a card—an ordinary, small, white card, slightly grubby, such as builders and decorators drop in at possibly promising addresses.

I still don't know what made me pick it up. I put down the mags, leaflets, ads for Rye Linen and Kids' Clothes and hold it in my hand and stare down. The dingy, stately home colours applied in the hall of the little house used by Henrietta as both shop and consultancy for interior design make it difficult to decipher who is trying to persuade us to buy what on this day, as fireworks and gloom and sudden squalls lift the children's pointed, fancy-dress witch hats right off their heads.

But there it is:

Tiles.

Provençal and Tuscan tiles fitted. Best quality.

And his name underneath. I can't help smiling at the amateurish writing and lettering on the card—it reminds me that Alain is French and probably can't read or write well in English.

But where is he?

The phone number, a mobile number, is painted in the right-hand corner of the card.

A cracker goes off outside, so I nearly jump out of my skin.

Emma Tennant

Henrietta's phone sits waiting on her desk messed up with unanswered letters and unpaid bills. What do I do?

Or Will He?
—What Would You Do?

♋ 36 ♋

A list of choices for aspiring Sugar Mummies. Endings—and maybe you'd like to add your own—are just as interesting as beginnings, if you come to think of it.

We're all near our own endings, we Sugar Mummies, and however much wrinkle remover we apply we'll soon be ready to join the other kind of mummy, the kind the British Museum has in its Egyptian department.

So this is how *Confessions of a Sugar Mummy* finishes—or is it?

Happy Ending

Hollywood makes a film of the book, showing Scarlett marrying Alain—after the sad death of his wife from a long illness. The extreme old age of the happy couple (Alain has caught up with our heroine by now) results in glowing references to Spencer Tracy and Kathleen Hepburn in *On Golden Pond*.

Unhappy Ending

As in *Love Story*, it has to be the girl who dies. Scarlett's sad demise is shown with supernatural lighting effects, so it is as a young woman that she leaves the grieving Alain to live out the rest of his days with his wife.

The Wings of the Dove Ending

᭦᭦   ᭦᭦

Scarlett — as Milly Theale—sells her flat for a colossal sum and then dies, leaving all her money to Alain. His wife Claire, however, cannot fail to observe Alain's new lack of love for her and accuses him of having fallen in love with the memory of Scarlett. He confesses and his marriage breaks up.

The Wings of the Dove, with a Twist

❧   ❧

Alain overdoes it on booze and drugs, and dies. Scarlett is heart-broken, but able to live in her flat to a ripe old age.